America is great because its people are good.
If the American people ever lose their goodness,
America will cease to be great.

—Alexis de Tocqueville, 1835

Sweet Land of Story
Thirty-Six American Tales to Tell

Pleasant DeSpain

Illustrated by Don Bell

August House Publishers, Inc.
LITTLE ROCK

Published 2000 by August House Publishers, Inc.
P.O. Box 3223, Little Rock, Arkansas, 72203,
501-372-5450.

Printed in the United States of America

10 9 8 7 6 5 4 3 2 1 HB
10 9 8 7 6 5 4 3 2 1 PB

LIBRARY OF CONGRESS CATALOGING-IN-PUBLICATION DATA
Sweet land of story : thirty-six American tales to tell / [compiled by]
Pleasant DeSpain ; illustrated by Don Bell.
    p.   cm.
Includes bibliographical references.
Summary: Thirty-six true, tall, and traditional tales, primarily from the
nineteenth century or earlier, selected by a professional storyteller and
divided by the region of the United States from which they originated.
ISBN 0-87483-569-0 (alk. paper)—ISBN 0-87483-600-X (pbk. : alk. paper)
1. United States—Literary collections. 2. Tales—United States.
[1. United States—Literary collections. 2. Folklore—United States.
3. Storytelling—Collections.] I. DeSpain, Pleasant. II. Bell, Don, 1935– ill.
PZ5 .S975 2000
398.2'0973—dc21   00-056543

Executive editor: Liz Parkhurst
Production editor: Joy Freeman
Copy editor: Jody McNeese Keene
Book designer: Joy Freeman
Cover and book illustration: Don Bell

The paper used in this publication meets the minimum requirements
of the American National Standard for Information Sciences—
Permanence of Paper for Printed Library Materials, ANSI Z39.48–1984.

AUGUST HOUSE   PUBLISHERS   LITTLE ROCK

for Bonnie E. DeSpain,
my courageous, kind, and loving
sister-in-law

Acknowledgments

This collection represents good American sharing at its best.

I appreciate fellow citizens from every region of this country who have generously shared their stories with me and have been willing to listen to mine .I'm extremely grateful to colleagues, loved ones, and friends who have shared my view that story can be used to embellish our past, enliven our present, and enlighten our future. Included are:

Eleanor J. and Edward E. Feazell, my mother and stepfather
Robert A. DeSpain, my father
The rest of my wonderful family
Members of other nurturing circles in my life:
Toby Marotta, Editorial consultant
Liz and Ted Parkhurst, Publishers
Don Bell, Illustrator
Jody McNeese Keene, Editor
Joy Freeman, Project editor
Leonard Scheff, a champion of this book from the start.
Brothers Sam and Jim Kephart, who made my move to New
    Hope nearly effortless
The Helene Wurlitzer Foundation of New Mexico(Taos)

I owe allegiance and appreciation to the following libraries, where I've spent countless hours exploring the story collections:

Tucson Public Library
University of Arizona Library
Seattle Public Library
University of Washington Library (Seattle)
Philadelphia Public Library
Bucks County Free Library (Doylestown, PA)
Birmingham Public Library
Princeton University Library
Denver Public Library

Contents

ROCKY MOUNTAIN

PACIFIC COAST

Introduction

In the early 1970s, shortly after setting out to become a professional storyteller, I was invited to tell tales at a communal gathering in Seattle. My agreed-upon fee was a massage and a vegetarian meal. Thirteen adults, seven children, and I gathered in the living room after dinner. I sat in front of their crackling fireplace. They settled into old couches, soft chairs, and fluffy floor pillows. I told a half-dozen stories that night and felt as though each had been truly heard.

A month later I was invited to return. No fee was mentioned, just dinner. When we reassembled in the large living room after the meal, my host announced, "We're the storytellers tonight, Pleasant. You're here to listen."

Two hours later, I'd heard a story from each person, including the children. Some of their tales were short. Others ran on. Some made me laugh. One made me cry. Some needed work. Others were polished. But each, in its own way, was a gem. Paid handsomely for my listening,

I realized then that we all have some kind of story worth telling.

Working as a professional storyteller, I travel in every state in this country, and I have found stories worth hearing and telling again in each. Surely my wanderlust has family roots. My great-great-grandfather, Pleasant DeSpain, Sr., was born in Kentucky in 1822. By oxen-pulled wagon he moved his family from there to Illinois and then Colorado. There he started a water and ditch company that helped hone Colorado's early water rights laws. The community he settled north of Denver has grown into a thriving suburb named Westminister, where a school and park are named for him.

Clearly our country's strength comes from wisdom born of dealing with our diversity in pioneering ways. The United States of America is the fourth largest country in the world. Only Russia, Canada, and China have larger land areas. Topographically, America's highest point is Mount McKinley, Alaska, at 20,320 feet. The lowest land-point is Death Valley, California, at 282 feet below sea level. Death Valley gave us our highest recorded temperature (134 degrees F.). Barrow, Alaska, provided the lowest (minus 80 degrees F.). The longest of our many rivers is the Missouri, at 2,540 miles. The largest of our scenic islands is the Big Island of Hawaii, at 4,038 square miles. The rich diversity of America's landscape characterizes her people and their stories as well.

For this, my seventh collection of tellable tales, I've selected thirty-six stories representing the six major regions of the United States. Each story was born as a child of the oral tradition. All have acquired meaning, shape, and voice through the process of being shared aloud. Now they are ready for broader horizons. Thanks to the "melting pot" nature of modern American culture, each meets the standards of universality and tellability.

The stories here reflect not only our pioneering past and our pride in accomplishment, but contemporary efforts to understand our culture. To illustrate our country's diversity, I've included tales that are silly and scary as well as practical and wise. The regional tales might seem like humble fare, but taken as a whole, the aim of this book is much more ambitious. Indeed, it can be seen as nothing less than a storyteller's portrait of our nation's character.

Tell these stories and tell them often. For in the end, after all, it's our stories that tell us who we are.

Pleasant DeSpain
New Hope, Pennsylvania
January, 2000

NORTHEAST

The Northeast formed the nucleus of the United States following the Revolutionary War of 1775–83. Steeped in history, this region laid a solid foundation for America's character.

My first teaching assignment, at the University of Massachusetts in Amherst, came in 1966. I was twenty-one, naïve, and a newcomer to the Northeast. Small New England towns sprouting white church steeples inspired me. Cascades of fall color astounded me. I lived in the small, historic town of New Salem, Massachusetts, and endured a cool reception by long-established neighbors. I was an outsider who had yet to prove himself. When asked to join the volunteer fire department some nine months later, however, I knew that I had at last been found worthy.

Hank Johnson, my closest New Salem neighbor, once said, "Life is hard, and it's worth it." These stories are born of surviving hardship and making one's way in the world. A nation's character is not assumed. It is earned.

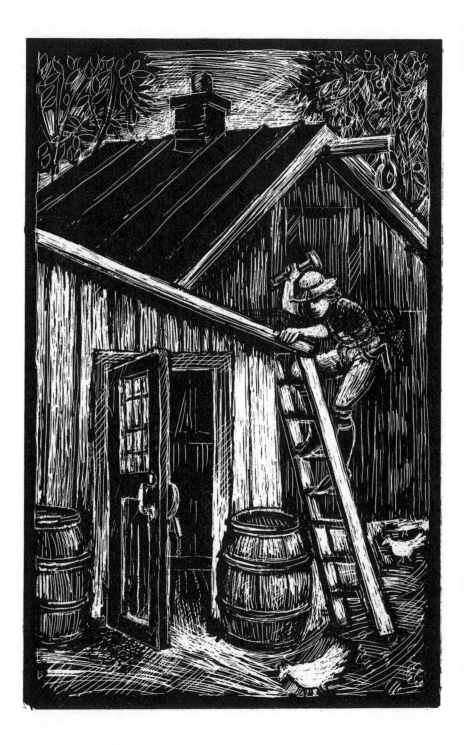

The Chicken-Coop Jail

Patriot or Tory? That was the question asked of every man during the Revolutionary War.

Would he support American freedom? Or would he join the Tory fight for loyalty to England?

Most early Americans, wanting their own government, fought as Patriots. A few, however, thought that the colonies should remain loyal to their English King George.

Nathan Jackson was a hard-working Yankee farmer who lived in Great Barrington, Massachusetts. A humble and honest man, he would often say, "I live in America, but I'm ruled by England. And that's the way it should be."

Nathan Jackson was a Tory, through and through.

When English ships landed on the American coast, he put on a red coat, picked up his musket, and joined the fight to subdue his countrymen.

When his own village came under assault, most of the English soldiers died or fled in defeat.

Nathan, however, was wounded in the leg and captured by his neighbors. He was placed in jail and charged with treason. The standard penalty for treason was death.

His village jail was nothing more than an old chicken

coop with two windows and a wobbly door without a lock. Escape would have been easy.

The local sheriff, also a farmer, was one of Nathan Jackson's neighbors. He said, "Tell me that you'll stay put, and I'll see to it that your leg is treated and that you're fed on time."

Nathan replied, "I've got no place to go, Sheriff. I was on the losing side of the battle. My farm's been seized. I won't run." But after two weeks in jail, Nathan was bored.

One morning he decided that he had to find something to do. Since his leg was mending, he could walk. When he limped outside, he discovered a pile of lumber and some hand tools behind the coop.

The sheriff wanted him to build a stronger jail. Nathan set to work, and by the end of the day, the coop was far more secure.

The sheriff was pleased and he asked if there was anything else Nathan wanted to help with.

"I'd like to plant and tend a vegetable garden on my former farmland."

"Will you come back to jail each night?" asked the sheriff.

"I will."

Nathan worked on his garden all throughout the summer and into the fall. Each night he returned to jail. The sheriff saw no need to find a lock for the door.

As the time for harvesting approached, the sheriff gave Nathan some news. "Your trial is to be held in Springfield next week, my friend. I must take you there myself. It's bad luck for both of us. You'll lose your life, and I'll lose my crops."

"Is there no one to help you with the harvest?" asked Nathan.

"No. Too many good men were killed in the battle. We farmers have been left to fend for ourselves."

"You've been good to me, Sheriff," said Nathan. "Better than I deserve. So you stay and harvest your crops. I'll walk to Springfield on my own."

"It's fifty-five miles from here," said the sheriff.

"I have a week. It will be my last walk. I'll enjoy it."

"Good thing I trust you," said the sheriff.

Early the next morning Nathan began his journey. Staying off roads as much as possible, he walked through fields, forests, and valleys. Delighting in the marvels of nature, he took note of every flower, tree, bird, and animal. He averaged eleven miles a day and slept in fields each night.

Eight miles from Springfield, back on the road for his last day of freedom, he came upon a horse-drawn carriage with a collapsed wheel. A distinguished-looking old man sat in the shade of a nearby tree. He was reading a large leather-bound book.

"Hail and well met, good sir," said Nathan. "I see you have a bit of difficulty."

"Yes, the wheel fell off, and I'm not strong enough to put it right."

"Two of us could do it. I'll lend a hand."

As soon as the wheel was back in place, the old man took out his wallet.

"Thank you, but no," said Nathan. "I won't be needing that."

"If you're going to Springfield, you must let me give you a lift."

"Now that's something I can use," said Nathan. "My feet are beginning to ache."

The old man became interested in his passenger. "Why are you headed for Springfield?"

Nathan told him the story. He mentioned the lost battle, the chicken-coop jail, and the sheriff who was reluctant to leave his ripened crops.

"And you're going to give yourself up to the court in Springfield?" the old man asked.

"Yes. I fought for the wrong side. Now I must suffer the consequences. It's only fair."

At the edge of town, Nathan jumped out of the wagon. "I want to walk this last bit. I hope you understand."

"Of course," the old man said. "I wish you well in court."

As good as his word, Nathan reported to the Springfield sheriff and was promptly put behind bars.

His trial was held the following morning. From behind the high bench, the local judge stared down at the accused. Then he solemnly intoned, "Nathan Jackson, you are guilty of the crime of treason. I sentence you to hang tomorrow morning."

With a sigh, Nathan dropped his head.

Suddenly, an elderly gentleman appeared from a side door. He wore a black robe and carried a large leatherbound book. It was the man that Nathan had met on the road.

Taking a seat one step higher than the local judge's chair, he said, "I'm the leader of the Governor's Committee sent from Boston. Last month we received a petition for clemency for Nathan Jackson. It was signed by many of Mr. Jackson's neighbors and sent to us by the sheriff of Great Barrington.

"They feel that he is a good and honest man who deserves another chance. I agree with them.

"Nathan Jackson, I set you free. Return to Great Barrington, burn your red coat, and be a good American from this day forth."

And he was.

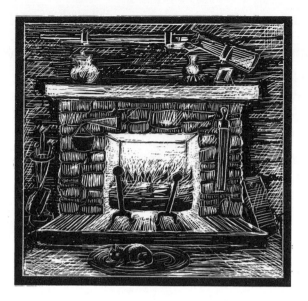

An Amazingly Long Time

A country gentleman named Squire Wadsworth kept his feelings to himself. His fifteen-year-old son, Weldon, had inherited the trait.

Late one winter afternoon, Squire Wadsworth told Weldon to go out to the woodpile and fetch a backlog for the hearth. Since the backlog keeps the fire burning throughout the night, it must be the largest log able to fit inside the fireplace.

Weldon was at an age when his father's orders resulted more often in swallowed anger than in ready compliance. Reluctantly, he put on his coat and walked through the snow to the woodpile.

He searched for a log of appropriate size but found nothing. The very thought of going to the barn for a handsaw to cut one made him rebel. So he grabbed the smallest log on the pile and carried it inside.

Without a word, he raked the coals forward and placed this miniscule stick at the back. His father watched from the comfort of his rocking chair.

Then the squire stood up, and without saying a word, he walked over to the wall and took down his razor-strap. "I'm without humor today, Weldon. Your joke is for naught. So go to the woodshed and fetch a proper log or your backside will burn hotter than the fire."

Weldon didn't flinch. Without saying a word, he walked outside, passed by the woodshed and continued onto the road. Not once did he look back.

He was gone for six years.

By the time he turned twenty-one, Weldon was full grown. He had made his way by becoming a black-smith's apprentice. Now he had his own forge. Since his arms were strong and his purse was full, he decided it was time to visit his father.

He arrived at Squire Wadsworth's house just as the sun was fading. When he peeked through a window, he saw his father, older and frailer, sitting in his rocking chair before the fire. Inspiration struck. He went to the woodshed and found the largest log in the pile. Then he hoisted it to his shoulder, walked into the house, and laid it in front of the hearth.

"Here's the backlog you wanted, Father."

Squire Wadsworth stared at the strapping young man who had just called him father with astonishment. Yes, he concluded, it was Weldon, gone for all these years.

A long moment passed as father and son looked each other over.

"You say that you've brought in the backlog?" the squire managed to ask.

"Yes sir, just as you ordered."

Another long moment passed.

"Well," the good squire mumbled. "It's taken you an amazingly long time to fetch it. Rake the coals forward, put the log on, and wash up for supper. Your mother is anxious to see you."

Agnes and Henry, a Love Story

MASSACHUSETTS

It began during the summer of 1742 in Marblehead, the smuggling port for Boston. Henry Frankland, a twenty-six-year-old Englishman, was sent to collect taxes on the contraband trade.

Henry came from a fine English family. He was blessed with high social status as well as immense personal wealth. Added to these gifts were exceptional intelligence and a handsome appearance. Happiness was his for the asking.

Agnes Surriage was a sixteen-year-old Puritan. Confident and beautiful, she worked as a serving maid at the Fountain Inn in Marblehead. When necessary, she scrubbed pots, never complaining about her long hours of labor.

The first time he saw Agnes, Henry Frankland's eyes grew wide. She was down on her knees, scrubbing the floor. His stare caused her to glance up. She smiled with genuine warmth. Smitten, he had no choice but to return the smile.

Agnes served Henry his dinner with lowered eyes. She answered his questions with a soft voice. Upon leaving the inn, he gave her a piece of silver and asked, "Will you be here tomorrow night?"

"I'm here every night. This is my appointed life."

He returned the following night and again the night after. With each visit he learned more of her history and saw more of her nature. Agnes had been born to poor, hardworking parents. She was well loved and loved her family in return. She accepted her position in the New England Puritan social order, believing that hard work brought lasting rewards.

In less than a week, Henry had met with her parents and asked their permission to move Agnes into his aristocratic Boston home. "She will be my ward," he said. "I'll provide her with fine clothing. She will learn proper speech and etiquette. She will have every educational advantage. I'll care for her to the best of my ability."

Her parents cried tears of joy.

Agnes proved worthy of Henry's trust. In a few years, she blossomed into a radiant young gentlewoman. When she turned twenty-one, they declared undying love for each other and vowed that they would one day be married.

Then Henry's uncle died, which presented a major obstacle. Henry inherited the baronetcy of the Yorkshire branch of the Franklands. Having no choice, he assumed his new title, Sir Henry Frankland, Baronet.

The obstacle was this: noblemen did not marry serving

maids—not in the British Isles, not in Puritan New England, not ever.

But he couldn't let her go. Nor could she live without him.

It wasn't long before indignant members of Boston society were whispering behind their backs. "She is his ward, or so they say." "Ten years his junior and his constant companion." "Unmarried! Have they no shame?"

Sir Henry built a new mansion on Hopkinton Island, many miles from the cruel city. They continued their life together in seclusion.

Happiness remained theirs for several years. The elegance of Sir Henry's house and the beauty of his life-companion became legendary throughout New England. Many disapproved of their living together, but no one interfered.

In 1755, the year of the great Lisbon Earthquake, Henry and Agnes traveled to Portugal. Henry was riding out of town on business when the quake struck. Falling walls crushed his carriage. Buried under piles of rubble, he struggled to survive.

Agnes had rushed from their hotel into the street as soon as the terrible shaking began. Running through their destroyed neighborhood in search of him, she called out his name over and over again.

Just by chance, on the third street over, she spotted a bloody hand in the sleeve of a fine jacket reaching up from a pile of stones. For hours, she labored to dismantle the premature grave. Finally she rescued her still-breathing Henry.

After finding a safe house, she nursed him back to health.

As soon as he recovered, Sir Henry and Lady Agnes were officially married. She gave him his life. He gave her his title. Such is the power of love.

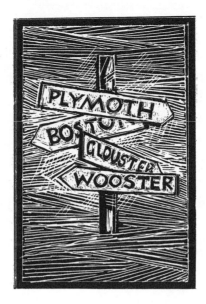

The Legend of Peter Rugg

NEW ENGLAND

In the early 1800s, William Austin rode by stagecoach from Providence, Rhode Island, to Boston, Massachusetts. Since the coach was full, he had to sit outside next to the driver. He found the driver an agreeable tour guide.

As they passed the ten-mile post, his team of horses pulled their ears back. "It's the storm-breeder," said the driver. "He'll pass us soon. Wherever he goes, a storm is sure to follow."

"There isn't a cloud in the sky," replied Austin.

"Storm-breeder isn't a cloud. In fact, here he comes now."

Heading toward them was a black carriage driven by a large man seated in a worn cane chair. At his side sat a small girl. A large black horse pulled their carriage. It approached the stagecoach without slowing down.

Austin noticed that the girl looked sad. Her companion's brooding eyes swept over them as their carriage passed the coach. As soon as those mysterious travelers had passed, the horses' ears stood back up.

There was a clap of thunder in the distance. Then came a downpour of rain. Austin and the driver got soaked. As swiftly as it had arrived, the storm passed.

Austin asked, "Who was that man—and how does he bring rain?"

"He's the infamous Peter Rugg."

"And the girl?"

"His child, Jenny."

"Have you seen them before?"

"I've passed them on the road nearly a hundred times over the years. He used to stop me, always asking the same question: 'Which road to Boston? I've lost my way and we must get home.' I don't bother to answer any longer, so he's stopped asking. But the rain still comes."

Three years later, when he checked into Bennett's Hotel in Hartford, Connecticut, William Austin heard a man on the hotel porch shout, "There goes Peter Rugg and his girl! They're drenched as always and farther from Boston than ever."

Austin ran to the porch. "Just who is this Peter Rugg?" he asked.

"A famous traveler," replied the stranger. "One cursed by heaven. He and his daughter have searched for Boston for many a year. They have yet to get there. It was fifteen years ago that he first approached me, asking for directions to the great city. I explained that he was headed the wrong way. I told him to turn around and go back one hundred miles.

"He didn't believe me. 'How can that be?' he demanded. 'I was told that Boston lay before me. Why do men deceive me? I've gone east, then west. I've followed the guideposts. I've turned back. I've headed south, then north. Why does the city hide from me? Why?'

"During the last fifty years, he's been seen on every road that leads to Boston. But he's never made it home."

Some years later Austin had the good fortune to meet an elderly Bostonian named James Felt. Mr. Felt and Peter Rugg had lived in the same neighborhood as children. At eighty years of age, Mr. Felt had an interesting story to tell.

"Peter Rugg—if he's still alive—would be seventy-nine. His daughter Jenny was ten at the time of the Boston Massacre in 1770. She'd be near sixty today. They lived on Middle Street. He had a foul temper, Peter did. Everyone knew to keep a distance whenever he got riled. His ranting and raving could wake the dead.

"Well, he and Jenny left for Concord one late autumn morning. He wanted to get back by nightfall. But there was a bone-rattler of a storm that night. No one should have been out in it, especially not a child.

"The following spring I went to Cambridge to talk with Mr. Cutter, one of Peter's friends. He told me that Peter and Jenny had stopped by on the afternoon of the big storm. To spare them the foul weather, he asked them to spend the night.

"Peter became enraged, saying, 'Let the storm come and come strong. I'll make it home this night. Nothing on earth or in heaven will stop me!'

"They didn't return to Middle Street that night. Or ever again."

The following year Austin heard a rumor regarding Rugg. One dark midnight, a toll collector on the Charlestown Bridge had tried to stop a man and child in a carriage. They had traveled over the bridge several times before, but never stopped to pay the toll. On this particular night, the collector stood in the middle of the bridge to enforce the stop.

When Rugg's carriage approached with great speed, the collector threw a three-legged stool at the horse. It passed through the animal's body and landed on the other side of the bridge. Once again the toll wasn't paid.

William Austin concluded that the mystery of Peter Rugg was a matter best left to heaven.

Others say that on stormy nights, Peter Rugg and his daughter can still be seen searching for the proper road to Boston.

The Dutchman's Inn

PENNSYLVANIA

Early one winter a New York peddler named Royce drove his team and wagon to Pennsylvania hoping to sell pots and pans. One of his horses threw a shoe on the outskirts of Lancaster County, forcing Royce to stop for the night. He took a room at the Dutchman's Inn while the local blacksmith looked after his horse.

The wind blew at gale force throughout the night. A rain squall turned to sleet, then snow, and then ice. The temperature dropped like a stone down a well. By morning, the peddler was marooned.

"Looks like I'll be staying a few days more," he said to the inn's proprietor, a gruff man named Efram.

"That you will," replied Efram. Since he had seen the peddler's purse and knew that he could pay, Efram was pleased.

The innkeeper was a money-grubber. "I'll have to

charge you a bit more for the room as the storm requires more wood in the fireplaces," he told Royce. "Good firewood doesn't come cheap."

Royce didn't argue.

"I must ask a little more for dinner as well, food being scarce as it is," said Efram.

"All right," said Royce. "But I'll need another blanket for my bed. Surely you won't charge me extra for that."

"Only a penny," he replied. "A penny more each night."

The storm lasted for five more days and Royce endured added charges at every turn. "I'm at his mercy," he thought. "But there's always a way to turn a curse into a blessing."

When the storm finally passed, Royce was eager to be on his way. "I'd like to settle my bill," he said to innkeeper.

"I trust that you'll agree with my accounting. I've taken care to be fair and exact. You owe five dollars."

The total should have been closer to four dollars, even with all the extra charges added in. Royce opened his purse, counted out five one-dollar bills, and handed them to Efram.

The innkeeper smiled and, after placing the money in a drawer, handed Royce a tall mug of cider. "It's on the house. My gift to you for the road ahead."

Royce thanked him and tasted the golden liquid. "It's an excellent cider," he said, "but would make an even better wine. A fine wine sells for much more than cider."

"Of course," Efram agreed, "but how is it possible to turn cider into wine?"

"It's a secret process taught to me by my father. It

requires special equipment, which I have in my wagon along with my wares."

"How much do you want for the equipment?"

"It's not expensive," explained Royce. "Five dollars at most. The secret to making it work costs a bit more. Twenty-five dollars, to be exact."

"How do I know this isn't a trick?"

"You're far too smart a man to be fooled by the likes of me," responded Royce. "I'll sell you both the equipment and the secret today. Pay me five dollars now. Since it takes a month for the cider to turn into wine, I'll stop back by on my return trip to collect the other twenty-five dollars. By then you'll be satisfied that it really works."

"That sounds reasonable," agreed Efram.

"But first I need to do a little test on the wood of your cider barrel," said Royce.

Efram led him down to the cellar and pointed out the proper barrel.

"It's nearly full," he stated. "Does your process turn all of it into wine?"

"That and a bit more," explained Royce. "The wood must be able to expand a little. Loan me your auger and I'll bore a hole."

Intrigued, Efram complied. Then he watched carefully as Royce bored a hole near the bottom of the barrel.

"Quick," said Royce, "plug the hole with your thumb."

Not wanting to lose a drop of cider, the innkeeper jammed his thumb into the hole.

Royce drilled a second hole on the other side of the barrel. As the cider poured forth, he said, "Plug this hole as well."

Efram's arms barely reached around the fat barrel, but he was able to force his other thumb into the new hole. Now he was hugging the barrel tight.

"Good," exclaimed Royce. "The test is proceeding effectively. You stay put and I'll get the equipment from my wagon."

Efram wasn't going anywhere. If he removed his thumbs, his cider was lost.

"By the way," said Royce, "I'm not happy with my bill. I'll need to make a correction."

The peddler went upstairs, removed five dollars from the innkeeper's drawer, and walked leisurely to the stable. There he paid the blacksmith, harnessed his team, and drove away.

In the bright morning sun, his pots and pans banged together as the wagon bounced over the rough road. He smiled at the sound and thought, "I won't be coming back this way for a long time to come."

Pulling the Rope

CONNECTICUT

In 1770, Samuel Forbes built a house and barn in Canaan, located in the northwest corner of Connecticut. Soon afterward he fell in love with Lucy, the daughter of a local farmer named Amos Pierce. Samuel asked Amos for permission to court his daughter. Amos didn't feel that Samuel was the right man for his Lucy. Permission was denied.

Lucy wasn't a typical girl. She didn't enjoy baking or household chores. She wasn't handy with a needle and thread. She never said, "I think so," or "Perhaps, if you think it best," or "Yes, dear, whatever you decide." And she hated to wear frilly dresses.

Lucy was a strong woman. She made her way in the world as well as any man. When she wrestled with her brothers, she left them lying in the mud. She pitched hay and built fences. She raced horses and hunted game. She said, "Yes, that's what we'll do," and "Trust me, I'll get it done," and "That's my decision and I'm sticking to it."

She was a force to be reckoned with.

Lucy was smitten with Samuel. She felt that he would make a fine husband and good father. Thus she was disappointed with her father's decision.

"Father," she said, "Samuel is a good man. I want him to court me."

"Daughter," said Amos, "I've already said no."

"I've decided to marry him, Father."

"Not while you live under my roof, Daughter."

"Thank you for making it plain, Father."

"Then you'll obey me and not see Samuel?"

"No, Father. I'll move from under your roof."

Lucy saddled her horse and rode to Samuel's farm. After discussing their situation, they decided to elope that very afternoon. In a buggy, they drove to New York State and found a justice of the peace to do the honors.

Then the newly married couple headed back to Caanan, imagining their life together.

"I hope you realize that no man will ever tell me what to do," Lucy said aloud.

"My dear," responded Samuel, "every husband must set the rules of his household."

"You can set all the rules you want. Just don't expect me to follow them."

"How will we get along together?" he asked.

"It will be best if I make the rules and you follow them," she answered.

"Is that fair?"

"I'm as strong as you are," she said. "I can run the farm

as well as you can. Why shouldn't I rule our roost?"

Samuel had an idea. "Let's have a contest of strength when we get home. If you win, you'll be in charge. If I win, the rules are mine."

"Agreed," said Lucy with a smile.

When they arrived home, Samuel tossed a long rope over the roof of his barn. One end hung down on the barn's right side. The other hung down on the left.

"You pull down from one side and I'll pull down from the other," he explained. "Whoever pulls the entire rope over the barn is the strongest. Do you agree, my love?"

"Yes, Samuel, I agree."

They took their places, and on his signal they began to pull. Lucy pulled with all her might and failed to yank the rope over to her side. Samuel pulled with all his strength and failed as well. Neither could best the other. The rope still straddled the barn's roof.

"Now, dear wife," hollered Samuel, "come round to my side of the barn. I have something to show you."

Lucy was curious, so she dropped her end of the rope and walked around to her husband.

He held out his end of the rope and said, "You grab hold as well. We'll pull together."

They did. The rope flew easily over the barn and piled at their feet.

"Let that be the way our house is run," said Samuel. "Let's pull together."

Lucy smiled. "You are wise, husband mine."

Working together, they prospered on the land, raised many fine children, and lived a long and happy life.

SOUTHEAST

Say the names slowly and hear the music: Carolina, Tennessee, Virginia, Appalachia. Along with elegant mansions, historic battlefields, and sweet-potato pie, the Southeast has a rhythm unto itself. There is time for story. Yesterday's hopes, defeats, and victories are alive today. Memory does not fade.

My great-great grandparents, Pleasant Sr. and Sarah DeSpain, were Kentucky-born. They worked hard and talked slow. Tintype photos from 1875 show them sitting rigid, unsmiling, staring hard at the camera lens. "We've earned our stories," they seem to say.

I've traveled throughout the Southeast over many years. Wherever I've stopped to share stories, I've taken time to listen as well. I've sat on porches and tuned my ears to Southern dialect. I've slowed my heart rate and enjoyed a lingering pace. I've come away with a sense of another time, another world. My soul was engaged.

The home of the National Storytelling Association is in Jonesborough, Tennessee. As it should be.

The Ghost Dog

Long ago, in the Allegheny Mountains, a spectral Labrador retriever was often seen at night. Some say that it happened on Virginia's Back Creek Mountain. Others say it was Brush Mountain, near Blacksburg. Wherever it took place, the story remains the same.

The ebony black dog was large and powerful. He appeared at sunset and prowled the mountain pass all night. No one knew what he was searching for. All agreed that he was a ghost.

Years went by, and his legend grew. Virginians spoke in whispers when discussing their encounters with the dog.

"I was setting up camp at nightfall," said a mountain man. "I'd just put a pot of rabbit stew on the fire when I heard a dog barking in the distance. I didn't think much about it. Then the barking got closer. Somehow it sounded sad. I remember thinking that it was a good thing that I was cooking up a sizeable pot of stew, because I was about to have company.

"I pitched my tent and waited for a stranger with a dog to hail me. But no one did.

"The barking continued. It got on my nerves. So I made a bright torch from a fallen branch and walked a few yards into the forest.

"That's when I saw him. Near scared me to death, him being so darn big. He looked me over careful-like and then growled, warning me to stay back.

"'Where's your master?' I asked. 'Fine dog like you can't be up on this mountain alone. Where's your master, I say.'

"The dog put his head up and wailed with a long, mournful howl. Near broke my heart. Then he trotted up the trail and my light couldn't hold him any longer. He vanished like a shadow in the night.

"When I got back home, I told my neighbor about it. He said it was the same dog he'd seen one night the summer before. He threw a rock at him, trying to get him to stop all that barking. He said the rock passed right through the dog's body. I thought maybe he missed him with the rock and didn't want to admit it. I changed my mind two years later.

"A highborn Englishwoman showed up at my cabin door in the early spring. The snows were melting fast and the mountain passes were ready for travel. She had a calm but sure way about her. She was searching for her husband who'd left his homeland years before. He wanted to settle somewhere in Virginia and was going to build a house and business before sending for his wife. He brought his dog with him, a full-grown black Labrador. They were mighty close, the man and dog.

"She got three letters from him during the first two years he was away. The last one said that he'd found a beautiful place to build and was settling the land deed. That was the last she heard. She waited a year, then sailed over here last summer. Been searching for him ever since.

"She described her husband as being tall and handsome with bushy eyebrows and wavy brown hair. Said he spoke with a strong English accent. Asked if I'd run into him.

"I said, 'No, but tell me about the dog. Maybe I've seen him.'

"A cold shiver ran up my spine as she went on to describe the dog on the mountain as exact as could be.

"We rode up to the pass late that afternoon and waited for nightfall. The wind picked up and I lit the lanterns. It wasn't long before we heard the barking and howling. It was pitch dark by the time the dog was close. He was scaring our horses. I made sure they were all right. Then I handed her a lantern and said, 'Follow me.'

"We walked the short distance to the very top of the pass, and there he was, standing in the middle of the trail. He growled softly and looked us over.

"She spoke first. 'Hunter, is that you? Are you really my Hunter Boy?'

"The dog began to wag his big tail with happy recognition. Then he came right up to her. She got down on the ground and threw her arms around his neck. He licked her face with his big wet tongue. Then she started to cry. She said, 'Where is he, Hunter? Where's my Cedric?'

"He looked at her with big sad eyes and trotted up the trail a bit. Then he stopped and looked back. She began to follow. Naturally, I followed her.

"Hunter led us to a pile of rocks not far off the trail and began to paw at the ground. The lady and I understood.

"After pulling the rocks away, we found the skeleton of a tall man. One bony finger bore a gold ring. She slipped it off and examined it.

"'I gave it to him the day we were married.'

"Hunter rubbed up against her and howled. Then he trotted back to the trail, and, like a wisp of smoke, faded into the night. He was never seen in those parts again.

"The Englishwoman sailed home with her husband's remains and gave him a proper burial. That was the last we heard about her."

The story of the faithful dog is still told in Virginia, and will likely be, for some time to come.

Poor Tail-eee-poe

Long ago, a man named Arlo lived in the backwoods of Kentucky, about a mile from Deadman's Swamp. He built a one-room cabin with a big front porch. The three bloodhounds he raised from pups liked to sleep under the porch. They were good hunting dogs, every one.

One day Arlo chopped a big load of firewood. It was hard work. His empty belly began to rumble and he doubled over in pain. It was a terrible hunger pain. He had the collywobbles.

He went inside and opened the cupboard. The shelves were bare.

Arlo grabbed his rifle and whistled for the dogs. They crawled from under the porch and started running and jumping and yelping all about the yard. They loved to hunt best of all.

They scoured the woods for two whole hours but

didn't have much luck. All they got was a tough old turkey-bird, just one.

The dogs wanted to go beyond the woods into the dreadful swamp. Arlo said, "No."

The mire and muck of the swamp reeked of danger. It oozed with quicksand and smelled like marsh gas. Arlo was sure that spirits and demons lurked in those slime pits. Their blood-curdling cries regularly shattered his calm. So he stayed out of the swamp and kept his hounds out of it, too.

The sun, all tuckered out after traveling across the sky, headed for the hills to bed down for the night. Swamp winds rose up like ghosts from a grave. A chill ran up Arlo's spine as he and his dogs hurried home.

While plucking the turkey-bird's feathers, Arlo heated water in a black pot hanging in the fireplace. Finding a sweet tater behind an empty flour sack, he cut it up for the pot. For flavor he added a big squirt of Kentucky Hot Sauce. Ummm-Mmmmmm! He cooked it all up and gobbled half of it down. The rest he gave to the dogs. He was still mighty hungry.

When it grew late, he put the dogs out and sat in the rocker in front of his fire. He rocked back and forth, forth and back. Flames sputtered and popped. His eyes drooped low.

Then suddenly he spied the shadow of a big, cat-like creature crawling along the wall.

Arlo's ax lay on the floor just below his hand. Slowly, he wrapped his strong fingers around the handle. With a jerk and a yell, he raised the ax high and flung it back down, chopping the tail of that thing right off!

With a scream the creature leapt through an open

window. It ran across the yard and headed into the
night-woods. For awhile the dogs barked and howled.
Then they crawled back under the porch.

Still shaking with fear, Arlo lit his lantern and looked
at the long fat tail on the floor. His belly ached with a
terrible hunger. On impulse, he put the tail in the pot
and cooked it up, adding a squirt of Kentucky Hot
Sauce for flavor. Ummm-Mmmmmm! He wolfed the
tail right down and at long last his belly was full.

Arlo yawned, blew out the lantern, and crawled into
his featherbed, which stood in the far corner of the room.
He pulled a patchwork quilt up to his chinny-chin, and
was soon asleep…in dreamland…for about an hour.

Then he awoke with a start. Something was crawling
on the cabin's roof. It was too big to be a squirrel. Arlo
listened hard, then shuddered. A grisly, scritchy-
scratchy voice said,

*Poooor tail-eee-poe. Where ohhh where is poooor tail-
eee-poe?*

"Get off my roof!" yelled Arlo.

The catamount leaped from the roof to the yard. The
three bloodhounds ran from under the porch and
chased it into a thicket on the edge of the woods. Then
it bounded out, paws hard on the ground, and they followed close behind. It led them further and further
away from the cabin, and closer and closer to the quag-
mire.

Arlo stood on his porch, listening to the dogs baying
and howling as they tracked the prey. Fearing for them,
he hollered, "Heeeeey dooooogs! Heeeeey doggieeees!
Come-on-hoooome, dogs!"

The hound dogs turned tail and ran home, panting

and slobbering. They crawled under the porch. The swamp-cat was gone.

Now Arlo was scared. He shuttered his windows and barred his door. Crawling back into bed, he tossed and turned for about an hour. Outside, in the eerie dark, pond frogs croaked and screech owls cried.

He jerked straight up. Something was on the porch. "Get away from here!" yelled Arlo.

The night sounds stopped. The grisly, scritchy-scratchy voice said,

Poooor tail-eee-poe. Where ohhh where is poooor tail-eee-poe?

Arlo hollered, "Get it, dogs, get it!"

The hounds weren't under the porch. They were waiting in a stand of trees on the far side of the yard. When the demon cat ran by, they leaped on it—and caught it!

It was a terrible fight. Fur was a-flying and dust was a-rising. Barking, yelping, screaming, and crying filled the night.

Suddenly the monster tore away from the dogs and ran into the woods. These bloodhounds were now as mad as they were mean. They stayed right behind it. They weren't going to lose it another time. The cat led them closer and closer to the boggy swamp.

Their barking got fainter and fainter. Then it stopped.

Arlo called out desperately, "Heeeere dogs! Heeeere dogs! Come on hooooome doggies!"

The wind, smelling of marsh gas, died down. Arlo knew the dogs had been run into quicksand. They weren't coming home ever again.

Arlo went inside. He found his hammer and a handful of rusty nails. From the inside he nailed the windows and door shut. Shaking like he had the fever, he crawled back into bed and pulled the patchwork quilt up to his chinny-chin. For about an hour he sweated and waited.

Then he sat up with a start. He rubbed his eyes and stared hard into the shadows. Evil was in the cabin.

Ever so slowly, it crept across the floor. Closer and closer to the foot of the bed it came. It had mean yellow eyes. It had sharp jagged teeth. It had long slashing claws. Arlo gulped.

With its grisly, scritchy-scratchy voice, it whispered:

Poooor tail-eee-poe. Here ohhh here is poooor tail-eee-poe.

"No!" cried Arlo. "No!"

"Yesss," it hissed. *"Poooor tail-eee-poe is mine!"*

The demon-cat jumped onto Arlo and ripped him apart.

That was a long, long time ago. But even today, Kentucky-folk tell strange and fearsome tales. They say that Deadman's Swamp is still a dreadful place, and that night winds still moan, full of sorrow. Listen close, and you'll hear a grisly, scritchy-scratchy voice,

Poooor tail-eee-poe. Here, ohhh here is poooor tail-eee-poe.

Caleb's Wild Ride

VIRGINIA

Caleb Johnson, a God-fearing, well-mannered, and studious lad of fourteen years, was in a quandary. It was a hot, humid summer Sunday morning. Church service meant two sweltering hours sitting on a hard pew while trying to stay awake. The nearby swimming hole promised heavenly relief from the sultry weather. The pond's calm, cool water, ringed with massive shade trees, called out, "Caleb, oh Caleb…"

"Are you ready for church, Caleb?" his mother hollered up the stairs.

"Yes, Ma," he answered. "But do we have to go? It's so hot."

"The way Satan likes it," she responded. "We have to be steady in the Lord just like every Sunday, hot or no."

"Yes, Ma."

Caleb clumped down the stairs, dragging his big feet

with each reluctant step. "I'm already sweating," he said.

"Quit complaining and let's go. We don't want to be late for Reverend Matthews's sermon."

Caleb and his mother walked the half-mile to church and mingled with the other parishioners on the scorched lawn before going inside.

Eddy, Caleb's best friend, tapped him on the shoulder. "Want to ditch out this morning?"

"How?" Caleb asked.

"Leave it to me."

Eddy walked over to Caleb's mother and said, "Morning, Mrs. Johnson. Is it all right if Caleb sits in the back with me today? I'll make him pay attention, I promise."

"As long as you both behave."

"Thanks, Mrs. Johnson."

The boys let everyone go into the church ahead of them. When the coast was clear, Eddy said, "Follow me," and ran into a nearby field, heading toward the swimming hole. Caleb shrugged his shoulders, yanked off his tie, and ran after his friend.

Since everyone else in town was in church, the boys had paradise to themselves. They took off their clothes and jumped in.

Ah, blessed relief. The cool water enveloped them in bliss. They splashed, swam, dunked each other, floated, and laughed.

Soon their laughter attracted a bull in the adjacent field. Large and territorial, he meandered to the edge of the pond and took a long drink.

"Is he dangerous?" asked Caleb.

"Nah, that's Farmer Tucker's bull. He means no harm."

The boys waded out of the pond and lay on the tall grass under a shady tree, drying off.

"Church is about over. We better get back," said Eddy.

"What will I tell my Ma when she asks me about the service?"

"Say 'good always overcomes evil.' It's what Reverend Matthews says every week."

Suddenly the boys heard a soft thump. When they looked down, they saw a large hornet's nest resting at their bare feet. A cloud of startled hornets flew out of the nest and began circling in the air. To escape the frantic insects, the boys leaped up and quickly climbed into the branches of the tree.

The hornets zeroed in on the bull, swarming over his massive horns. With a loud grunt, the bull lowered his head and ran straight for the tree. When he hit it—with a resounding *smack*—he knocked Caleb off his branch and onto the bull's back. Gripping its sides with his knees, he grabbed a horn with each hand.

Thus began Caleb's wild ride through the field and toward the church. Half of the angry hornets flew after the boy on the bull. The other half stayed with the boy in the tree.

Eddy leaped from his branch and ran after Caleb while batting the insects away with his hands. He didn't stop to consider that he, too, hadn't had time to get dressed.

The congregation gathered on the lawn saying their farewells. They heard it coming before they saw the unfolding spectacle.

The hornets stung! The bull bellowed! The boys

hollered! On they came, running right toward the parishioners. Eyes opened wide and jaws dropped low.

A strong fence at the back of the church stopped the bull's forward charge. Caleb jumped to the ground and fought off the last of the hornets. Eddy ran up, leaped over the fence, and crouched down, hiding on the other side. Caleb followed his friend over the fence.

With Caleb's astonished mother in front, the crowd slowly moved toward the fence. Farmer Tucker walked over to his bull, calmed him down, and led him home. Reverend Matthews had the good sense to run down to the pond and retrieve the boys' clothes. He tossed them over the fence, and two well-stung and embarrassed lads got dressed.

Caleb's mother asked one question on the long walk home. "What did you learn today?"

"Good always overcomes evil" was his sheepish reply.

Old Joe and the Carpenter

NORTH CAROLINA

Old Joe lived way out in the countryside all by himself. His best friend was also his closest neighbor. It seemed that they had grown old together. Their wives had passed on. Now that their children were raised and living lives of their own, all they had left were their farms...and each other.

For the first time in their long friendship they'd had a serious disagreement. It was a silly argument over a stray calf that neither one of them really needed. The calf was found on the neighbor's land, so he claimed it as his own.

But Old Joe said, "No, no. Now that calf has the same markings as one of my cows. It belongs to me!"

They were stubborn men. Neither would give in. Rather than hit each other, they stopped talking, stomped off to their respective doors, and slammed them shut! And that was that. Two weeks went by without a word between them. Old Joe was feeling poorly.

Come Saturday morning, Joe heard a knock on his front door. He wasn't expecting anyone and was surprised to find a young man who called himself a "traveling carpenter" standing on his porch. There was a wooden toolbox at his feet and kindness in his eyes.

"I'm looking for work," he explained. "I'm good with my hands, and if you have a project or two, I'd like to help out."

Old Joe replied, "Yes, as a matter of fact, I do have a job for you. See that house way over yonder? That's my neighbor's house. You see that creek running along our property line? That creek wasn't there last week. He did that to spite me! He hitched a plow to his tractor and dug that creek-bed from the upper pond right down the property line. Then he flooded it! Now we got this creek to separate us.

"I'm so darn mad at him! I've got lumber in my barn, boards, posts, everything you'll need to build me a fence—a tall fence—all along that creek. Then I won't have to see his place no more. That'll teach him!"

The carpenter smiled. "I'll do a good job for you, Joe."

The old man had to go to town for supplies. He hitched up his wagon and left for the day.

The young carpenter carried the lumber from the barn to creek-side and started to work. He worked hard and he worked fast. He measured, sawed, and nailed those boards into place all day long without stopping for lunch. As the sun began to set, he put his tools away. The project was complete.

Old Joe pulled up, his wagon filled with supplies.

When he saw what the carpenter had built, he couldn't speak. It wasn't a fence. Instead, a beautiful footbridge with handrails and all reached from one side of the creek to the other.

Just then, Old Joe's neighbor crossed the bridge, his hand stuck out. "I'm right sorry about our misunderstanding, Joe. The calf is yours. I want us to go on being good friends."

"You keep the calf," said Joe. "I want us to be friends, too. The bridge was this young fellow's idea. I'm glad he did it."

The carpenter hoisted his toolbox onto his shoulder and started to leave.

"Wait," said Joe. "You're a good man. My neighbor and I know everyone in the valley. We can keep you busy for weeks."

The carpenter smiled and said, "I'd like to stay, Joe, but I can't. I have more bridges to build."

And he walked on down the road, whistling a happy tune as he went.

Sam Davis and the Hangman's Noose

TENNESSEE

Sam Davis, a Confederate soldier, had a simple choice to make on the cold bleak morning of November 27, 1863: give up the name of his commanding officer and go free, or refuse to answer and climb the steps of a makeshift gallows. He was twenty-one years old.

The educated son of a wealthy plantation owner, Sam had a lot to live for. He had enrolled in military school as a boy. In 1861, when the Civil War began, he signed on with Company One of the First Tennessee Regiment of Volunteers. Six months later he was in West Virginia fighting under the commands of Robert E. Lee and Stonewall Jackson.

When Union armies captured Nashville, Sam's outfit was sent back to Tennessee. In the spring of 1862, he fought in the Battle of Shiloh. By now, he was a twice-wounded veteran. It was due to his intelligence, battle experience, and bravery that he had been assigned to Coleman's Scouts.

The Scouts were actually spies who investigated northern troop movements. Captain H. B. Shaw was their leader. He used Coleman as his cover name and passed as a doctor so that he could travel freely behind enemy lines. He personally had recruited Sam Davis as one of his aides.

Sam was on a scouting mission in Tennessee when he had received orders to go to Chattanooga. Two riders of the Seventh Kansas Cavalry captured him near the Alabama State line. The Seventh Cavalry were called Jayhawkers, and their sole assignment was to destroy Coleman's Scouts.

When the Jayhawkers searched Sam, they found detailed maps of northern troop locations under his shirt. They discovered a secret letter from Coleman to Confederate General Braxton Bragg in his boot.

General Grenville Dodge of the Sixteenth Federal Army Corps had Sam brought to his headquarters.

Each time he questioned Sam, General Dodge asked him to reveal Coleman's identity. "You're a young man," he said, "and you don't realize the danger you're in."

Sam replied, "I do know the danger of my situation, sir. And I'm willing to take the consequences. There is no power on earth that can make me tell."

Sam was allowed to write a letter home.

Dear Mother,

Oh, how painful it is to write to you! I have got to die tomorrow morning—to be hanged by the

Federals. Mother, do not grieve for me. I must bid you goodbye forevermore. I do not fear to die. Give my love to all.

Your Son,
Sam Davis

P.S. Mother, tell the children all to be good...Father, you can send after my remains if you want.

On November 27, a drum roll greeted the dawn. Sam's hands were cuffed behind his back. He was forced to sit on his own coffin in the rear of a wagon. Captain Armstrong, the officer in charge of the execution, ordered his troop to accompany the wagon to Seminary Hill. There a noose hung heavy from a scaffold beam.

Captain Armstrong looked worried. Sam said, "I do not think hard of you, Captain. You are doing your duty. What news from the front?"

He was told that General Bragg's troops had been defeated at the Battle of Missionary Ridge.

"I'm sorry to hear it, Captain. The boys will have to fight on without me."

Sam climbed the scaffold steps.

Suddenly a Kansas cavalryman appeared on the horizon, riding swiftly toward the gathering. He leaped from his horse and ran up to the scaffold, yelling, "Give up the name and you are a free man; General Dodge's orders."

Sam hesitated, then said, "I cannot. I had rather die a thousand deaths than betray a friend—or be false to duty."

The noose was placed over his head and tightened around his neck. Captain Armstrong gave the signal. The trapdoor opened, and Sam Davis died.

Along with a neighbor, Sam's younger brother, Oscar, brought the body back home. It still lies in the family cemetery.

A bronze statue of Sam has been erected on Nashville's Capitol Hill. The poet Ella Wheeler Wilcox penned these lines:

> Out of a grave in the Southland
> At the just God's call and beck
> Shall one man rise with fearless eyes,
> With a rope around his neck.

The Big, Smelly, Hairy Toe

NORTH CAROLINA

A man walked through the woods one day in search of things to eat. He spied a handful of acorns and put them into his sack. He found some mushrooms growing under a tree and put them into his sack. He stumbled upon a patch of wild onions and put them into his sack. He dug some red worms from the riverbank and put them into his sack. Then he came upon a giant, smelly, hairy toe half buried in a muddy hole. He picked it up and put it in his sack.

The man walked back to his cabin on the other side of the woods. He was hungry and looked forward to a tasty stew. He started a fire in the fireplace and filled a big black pot half full of water. When the water began to boil, he poured the sack's contents into the pot. He poured in the acorns. He poured in the mushrooms. He poured in the wild onions. He poured in the red worms.

And he poured in that big, smelly, hairy toe.

He cooked and stirred and stirred and cooked. He added salt and pepper and pepper and salt. He added three small carrots and one large sweet potato. The stew began to simmer. Earthy odors of woods and meadows filled the cabin. His stomach began to growl.

"Time to eat!" he said.

Slurp, chew, gobble, and swallow…down it went, with a big "yum, yum, yum!" His belly was full and he was tired.

"Yawn, yawn, yawn," he said. "Time for bed."

The man crawled into his big feather bed and pulled the green wool blanket tight around him.

"Snore, snore, snore," he said.

The night wind began to howl. The shingles on his roof rattled. The shutters on the windows banged. The door began to shake.

He woke up and heard a voice floating down the cold dark chimney and into the cabin.

"Who, oh who, has my big, smelly, hairy toe? I left it in the woods, but now it's gone. Who has it?…

"You?"

The man jumped out of his bed and with a shivery voice said, "Not me, not me! I have ten toes and none of them are hairy. Go away and leave me be."

The voice rattled the window.

"Who, oh who, has my big, smelly, hairy toe? I left it in the woods, but now it's gone. Who has it?…

"You?"

"Not me, not me! Two of my toes are big, and some of them are smelly. Go away and leave me be!"

The voice moved from the window and shook the door.

"Who, oh who, has my big, smelly, hairy toe? I left it in the woods and now it's gone. Who has it?...

"You?"

"Not me, not me! I have ten toes and all of them are smelly. Two are big but none of them are hairy. Go away and leave me be!"

The wind blew harder. The door flew wide open. A giant head with two blood-red eyes and a crooked grin peeked in. The creature's body was too big to fit through the door.

He slipped his enormous right foot onto the floor. The big toe was missing.

"Who, oh who, has my big, smelly, hairy toe? I left it in the woods and now it's gone. Who has it?...

"You?"

A big hand came through the door and one long crooked finger pointed to the man's foot.

The man followed the finger with his eyes. His very own big toe was growing bigger! His bigger big toe was growing hairier! It was also growing smellier!

The creature smiled. Then in came a hand holding a carving knife. He cut off the man's big, smelly, hairy toe. Then he placed it back on his own foot, and ran into the forest.

The man looked down at his bloody foot. He began to cry.

And ever since, he himself has wandered the dark woods, stopping at every cabin he finds, saying,

"Who, oh who, has my big, smelly, hairy toe? Who has it?...

"You?"

GULF STATES

The Gulf Coast plains dominate this unique region. Vast plains, low hills, and flat prairies create humid summers and mild winters. Rivers named Mississippi, Red, Tombigbee, and Rio Grande refresh parched lands and mark boundaries. This is the land of Lone Star, Dixie, magnolias, and pelicans. The stories told here are old, tall, and often true.

My first ocean sighting was in Galveston, Texas, in 1954. I was ten. My mother says that when I looked out upon the Gulf of Mexico, my eyes grew big and I went into a state of trance. "It was one of the rare times that you were truly speechless," she reminds me. This was after traveling from Denver to Fort Worth by train. This was after traversing Texas from Fort Worth to Galveston by automobile. So much empty land, so much open sea. My imagination soared.

I've traveled and told tales in Texas, Alabama, Louisiana, and Mississippi many times in the past thirty years. My memory holds sweltering summer heat, salty coastal air, and glass after tall glass of iced tea. And stories.

Pecos Bill

It's said that Pecos Bill, the greatest cowboy ever, was born in east Texas about 150 years ago. His daddy must have been a liar because the stories about Bill are hard to believe. His adventures are too tall for truth-telling but just right for a good yarn. Sit a spell and I'll tell you how Little Bill grew up to be so darned big and strong and downright mean.

Bill's family moved west by wagon train when he was just a baby. While the train was wading across the Pecos River, the little tot fell out of the wagon and float- ed downstream for ten miles. That's how he got his name. His folks searched high and low for him but didn't have any luck.

Coyotes found Baby Bill on the riverbank. Instead of eating him, they adopted him. So Bill learned how to yip and bark and howl with the best of them. He became a great hunter. After a few years, Bill thought he *was* a coyote.

One day, when the lad was nearly twelve years old, an old trapper paddled his canoe down river and came upon a marvelous sight. Bill was standing his ground in a meadow, fighting off three grizzly bears at the same time. When the bears charged at the boy, he threw dirt clods into their eyes, blinding them for a spell. Then he got the bears to turn on each other and let them fight to the finish.

When all three were dead, he built a big fire and cooked them up for dinner. He offered the trapper one, because two bears at one sitting was Bill's limit.

The trapper said, "You look like a heathen, boy. What are you doing running around without no clothes?"

"I'm not a heathen," said Bill, "I'm a coyote."

"No, you're not a coyote," said the trapper.

"Sure I am," replied Bill. "I can bark and I've got fleas. And I always howl at the moon."

"That don't prove a thing," said the trapper. "Most Texans have fleas. And I've heard lots of them bark and howl, especially on full-moon nights. You're not a coyote, you're a Texan."

"In that case," said Bill, "I'd better go to town and get some clothes and practice being a Texan."

Always a fast learner, Pecos Bill was soon acting like a real Texan. He snarled big and loud. He spit on clean floors. He drew his six-shooter faster than a bee could sting. He killed bad men without blinking an eye. And he liked to brag a bit, too. But not too much—Texans never have to brag too much.

Several years went by and Pecos Bill became famous for killing all the bad men in west Texas. He also rode cyclones without a saddle and lit his campfires with bolts of lightning. Naturally, he used just the little bolts.

One day Bill got bored and decided to travel further West for bigger adventures. He met an old cowboy near the New Mexico state border and said, "I'm looking for the meanest, rottenest, and toughest outfit I can find. I want to join up with the most worthless bunch of men in the West."

"Yer headed in the right direction, partner," replied the cowboy. "Ride up this trail for about a hundred miles and you'll meet up with the hardest gang of outlaws ever to rob a bank. They are so tough that they sprinkle gunpowder on their eggs for breakfast. They are so mean that they'll shoot a man if he so much as smiles. They are so ugly that women faint and children scream when they see 'em. But be careful, stranger. The boss man of that outfit is seven feet tall and as strong as a locomotive chugging up a steep hill. And he's the meanest one of all."

"Let me at 'em!" cried Pecos Bill, and he spurred his trusty horse on up the trail. Unfortunately, he was riding a little too hard and fast. His horse stepped into a gopher hole and broke its leg.

Now afoot, Bill slung his saddle and bridle over his shoulder and hiked up a hill. Suddenly he heard a rattlesnake a-rattlin'. It was a big one: ten feet of snake and two feet of rattles.

Bill always fought fair, so he put his saddle and rifle down and let the snake bite him a couple of times just to get things started. Then Bill lit into that rattler with both fists and one boot. He stepped on his tail. Then he boxed his head until all the poison was knocked clean out of him.

The rattler begged for mercy. Bill let him live. He simply wrapped the big snake around his neck like a thick scarf on a cold day.

Fifty miles on he came to a hidden canyon. When he sat down on a rock to rest for a spell, he laid the snake and his saddle on the ground.

Bill didn't see the mountain lion in the tree above.

This catamount was no puny, hardly-bigger-than-a-house-cat feline. It was a monster cat, as big as a long-horned steer and just as heavy. Its claws were as long as a pick-ax. Its teeth were as sharp as a straight razor. And it was hungry.

With a scream the mountain lion leaped from the tree onto Bill's back. Pecos didn't want to make a fuss, so he let the cat scratch and bite him for a few minutes. Then he tangled with the cat something serious. First he grabbed the critter by the neck and pulled out handfuls of fur. Then he hugged it around its middle so hard that the lion squeaked. Then he boxed his head with both fists until the mountain lion saw stars, started to cry, and begged him to stop.

Bill slipped his horse-bridle over the lion's head and threw his saddle over its back. After cinching the saddle down tight, he jumped on, figuring he'd learn how to ride a cat in no time. With a yowl, the catamount leaped into the air trying to shake Bill loose, but the Texan held on. Then he took his rattlesnake by its tail and whipped the cat. Down the canyon they went, a-hollering and jumping and rattling. Bill was having a grand old time!

They soon reached the ranch house of the wild bunch that Bill was looking for. The cowboys had never seen a bucking wildcat before, so they were a-might scared. Pecos Bill grabbed an ear to settle his lion down and jumped to the ground. He wrapped the snake back around his neck and walked over to the outdoor cook-stove.

A pot of beans made with hog fat was cooking on the fire. Bill grabbed the pot with his bare hands and poured the whole steaming stew down his throat. Next came their entire pot of boiling coffee to wash it down. With a prickly pear cactus he wiped his mouth clean. Then he asked, "Okay, who's the boss man of this here outfit?"

A giant of a man carrying two rifles, three pistols, and a bowie knife strapped to his waist stepped forward. He looked Pecos Bill right in the eye and growled, "I was, stranger. But now it looks like *you* are."

The Bluebonnet

COMANCHE/TEXAS

Four seasons passed without rain. Springtime was coming. The grass had turned to dust and a terrible drought was upon the land. The deer and the buffalo were dying. The people dug for edible roots to keep their families alive.

The Great Spirits did not hear the cries of hungry children. The Great Spirits did not hear the prayers of desperate men and women. The Great Spirits did not hear the chants of medicine men.

The Great Spirits had turned away because of a terrible wrong. The wrong must be made right. Only then would the life-giving rain of forgiveness fall.

"What is our great wrong?" the people asked.

The oldest shaman shook his seed rattles and began to dance. Around the fire he shuffled and chanted. He circled and sang sacred songs. Warriors beat their drums.

Women and children fell in around him. The entire village spoke with one voice, "How do we make it right?"

Finally the shaman screamed and fell to the ground. The Great Spirits had answered. He knew what to say.

The children helped him up. The women gave him water. Then everyone stood in silence to listen.

"We have been selfish. We have taken from our Earth Mother but haven't given back. Now we must give back. The Great Spirits ask for a sacrifice. We must burn our most-loved possession. It must be the finest thing in our village. The ashes of this offering are to be shared with the four winds, North, East, South, and West. Only then will we be forgiven. Only then will rain come."

The old men and women heard and understood. The young men and women heard and understood. The children heard and understood. They must give up their most-loved thing. What was it?

"It should be my grandfather's bow," said a warrior, "handed down to my father and then to me. I was going to give it to my son."

"It should be my beaded moccasins," said a woman. "It took two winters to make them."

"It should be the buffalo rug I love so much," spoke an old man. "It keeps me warm on cold nights."

"It's late and we are tired," said the shaman. "Tomorrow, when the sun is highest, we will decide."

The people returned to their teepees. Now they would dream of what they loved most. One little girl couldn't sleep. She was certain that she owned the finest possession of all. She knew that the Great Spirits had meant her doll.

It was no ordinary doll. It was a proud and fierce warrior made of soft buckskin. The rugged face was painted with the juice of berries. The loincloth and leggings were decorated with seeds and bone. A curved wooden bow was sewn in one hand, and a tiny beaded quiver was slung over its back. The blue war bonnet was made from feathers of the bird that cries "jay-jay-jay."

The girl hugged her little warrior doll. Her mother had made it for her after the death of her father. It resembled him. She didn't know if she could let go of the most precious thing in her life. Yet that's exactly what the Great Spirits had asked.

A coyote howled. A camp dog barked and was shushed. Crickets sang the village into ever-deepening sleep. The girl's mother began to snore. The time to act was now.

She crawled out of her teepee and crept up to the council fire. Under the cover of ashes, a single stick glowed red. She held up the firestick and blew on it. A flame burst forth. She carried it to the top of a nearby hill, then stooped to gather a small pile of twigs and branches.

She stood up and gazed at the vast, moonless sky. In one hand was her warrior doll. In the other was her homemade torch.

"Give me a sign, Great Spirits. Tell me that what I'm about to do is right."

A brilliant star streaked across the sky and fell below the horizon. This was her sign.

She thrust the burning stick under the branches and a fire took hold. Gently she laid her father-doll on the flames. Her eyes filled with tears as she said goodbye.

Flames flared. The twigs crackled. Her doll was reduced to ashes. When they were cool, she scattered them to the North, the East, the South, and the West. Then she lay down beside the cold fire and slept peacefully until morning.

The moment the sun rose she rubbed her eyes open and looked upon a new world. Everywhere the ashes had fallen, there were beautiful flowers dancing in the morning breeze. Their blossoms were as blue as the feathers of the bird that cries "jay-jay-jay."

It began to rain. People bolted out of their teepees, ran up the hill, and marveled at the spectacle. The shaman took the girl aside and asked her to explain. After hearing her story, he spoke to the people.

"Because of this girl's actions, the drought has ended. The Great Spirits have forgiven us.

"This brave daughter will have a woman's name. From this day forward, we will call her One-Who-Loves-Her-People."

The following year, birds, winds, and rains carried the seeds of the flowers to every hill, valley, and riverbed. And so it happens every year that the sacrifice of One-Who-Loves-Her-People gives Texas its brilliant bluebonnets.

Salting the Pudding

ALABAMA

Old Mrs. Simpson had the reputation of being a mighty fine dessert maker. Her apple pies and oatmeal cookies were the best in town. Her chocolate cake made mouths water for miles around. But it was her pudding that made grown men weep.

Mrs. Simpson had the magic touch when it came to making pudding. Even the local preacher, Reverend Higginbotham, called it "nectar and ambrosia in the same dish!"

Mrs. Simpson had five daughters. Each was old enough to help out in the kitchen. She let them mix the batter for her cakes and slice apples for her pies. She let them bake her oatmeal cookies. But when it came to pudding, she would shoo them right out of the kitchen.

"Too many cooks spoil the broth," she liked to say.

Claire and Christine, Mrs. Simpson's oldest girls,

were twins. She decided to have a big party for their birthday. Everyone in town was invited and also the preacher, who the Sunday before had praised her desserts from his pulpit.

Early that Saturday morning Mrs. Simpson set to work. With the help of her daughters, she made several delicious treats.

"Now it's time to clean the house, girls," she said. "Then I'll make the pudding."

The hour grew late. She finished just in time to go upstairs and put on her new store-bought dress.

While brushing her hair she remembered something. In all the excitement she had forgotten to salt the pudding.

Truly great pudding requires just a teensy pinch of salt. She had already taught her daughters this secret, and she knew that any one of them could help out.

"Claire, honey, go salt the pudding for me. I plum forgot," she yelled down to the oldest twin.

"Can't do it, Maw," she hollered back. "I'm polishing the dining room table. My hands are full of wax."

"Be a love, Christine, and salt the pudding," she told her second oldest.

"No, Maw, I'm tying ribbons in my hair."

"Faye, sweetie, go salt the pudding for your mother."

"Not now, Maw, I'm too busy ironing my dress," said the middle child.

"Then the job is yours, Irene my pretty," she said to the fourth daughter.

"Wish I could, Maw, but I'm doing the dusting."

"Mary Beth, you're my angel. Salt the pudding."

"Oh Maw, not now. I'm writing a poem for my teacher," said the youngest.

Mrs. Simpson sighed long and loud. "Five daughters and not one can lend a hand." She finished dressing, went down to the kitchen, and carefully salted the pudding.

Claire finished her polishing and slipped into the kitchen to wash her hands and salt the pudding.

Christine tied the final ribbon in her hair and skipped down to the kitchen to salt the pudding.

Faye put on her freshly ironed dress and stopped by the kitchen to salt the pudding.

Irene stashed her dusting rag in the kitchen closet and, since she was there, salted the pudding.

When Mary Beth wrote the last line of her poem, she knew it was time to do what her mother had asked. So she, too, tiptoed into the kitchen and salted the pudding.

Mrs. Simpson put the pudding in to bake just as people began arriving for the birthday party. Music, dancing, laughter, and all kinds of delicious treats were enjoyed. But everyone was awaiting the famous pudding.

Mrs. Simpson removed it from the oven. She let it sit a spell before carrying it into the dining room. It looked perfect. It smelled divine. Mouths began to water and lips started to smack in anticipation of the taste to come.

"Preacher Higginbotham," she said proudly, "you be the first."

"Mrs. Simpson," he replied, "this will be as close to heaven as I'll get here on earth."

With the largest spoon on the table, he dug in. He paused to let his big mouthful of flavor soak in. Then his eyes narrowed. His face wrinkled up. First came a look of shock, then finally, disgust. He spat it out onto the floor.

Everyone gasped! Mrs. Simpson looked dumbfounded. Then she put her finger into the pudding and took a taste. Crinkling up her nose, she looked at her daughters and demanded, "Which one of you salted the pudding?"

"I did," said all five in unison.

"And so did I." She laughed. "See, too many cooks not only spoil the broth, they ruin the pudding!"

Strongest of All

LOUISIANA

One day long ago, clever Rabbit was walking along the seashore. Hearing voices, he stopped to listen. Elephant and Whale were having a conversation. He wanted to hear every word.

"Sister Whale," said Elephant, "you are the largest, strongest, and most beautiful animal of the sea. Naturally, I'm the largest, strongest, and most beautiful animal on the land. We two should rule over all the animals, birds, and fish on the earth."

"Yes, it's true, Brother Elephant," said Whale. "We are the greatest. You should rule the land. I'll be happy to rule the sea."

Rabbit decided to play a trick on these two behemoths.

"I'm twice as smart as both of them," he said. "All I need is a long, strong rope and my jungle drum."

Later that afternoon Rabbit found Elephant in the

woods and said, "Hello, Powerful Ruler of All the Animals that Walk and All the Birds that Fly. I'm in need of a small favor."

Elephant liked Rabbit's compliment and was willing to listen.

"What can I do for you, my little friend?" he trumpeted.

"My milk-cow is stuck in the sand on the beach. I'm not big enough to pull her out. Let me tie one end of this rope around you and the other end around my cow. When you hear me beat my drum, you'll know it's time to pull hard, really hard."

"It's a good plan," said Elephant. "You are wise to come to me as I'm the strongest friend you have."

"Thank you, Elephant. Wait for the drum!"

So saying, Rabbit ran to the beach and found Whale sunning herself near the shore.

"Hello, Friend Whale. My, but you look sleek and powerful today," said Rabbit.

Whale smiled and replied, "Yes, Rabbit, I'm strong today and every day. I rule all the creatures of the sea."

"Of course," responded Rabbit. "That's why I've come to you with my small problem."

"What can I do to help?" asked Whale.

"It's my milk-cow. She's mired deep in the bayou-mud way up in the woods. I can't get her out. I'd like to tie one end of this rope around your tail and the other end around my cow. I'll beat my drum so you'll know when to pull."

"Of course I'll help," said Whale.

She swam closer to shore so that he could tie the long rope to her massive tail.

"Pull hard when you hear my signal," said Rabbit as he ran back into the woods.

He found his drum and pounded hard and loud. *Boom! Boom! Boom!* The sounds carried to both Elephant in the forest and Whale in the sea.

They both began to pull, each against the other, and were shocked at the resistance. Elephant tugged so hard that Whale hit the sand in the shallow water. Whale pulled back so hard that Elephant was being dragged out of the woods.

"That cow must be stuck in the sand up to her neck," bellowed Elephant.

"That cow must be buried in the mud up to her nose," cried Whale.

Next thing they knew the rope snapped! One end flew back and stung Elephant on the ear.

"Ouch!" he cried.

The other end smacked Whale on the tail.

"Ouch!" she cried.

Rabbit began to laugh. His laughter carried deep into the woods and far out to sea. Elephant and Whale realized that they had been tricked. They also discovered that when it came to cleverness, Rabbit was the strongest of all.

Sam Bass

TEXAS

Even though he was an outlaw, Sam Bass was well liked. The folks of Denton County called him the Robin Hood of Texas.

Born in 1851, he traveled from Indiana to the Lone Star State when he was twenty-one. For the next five years he made his living by gambling on racehorses.

Sam became an outlaw at twenty-six. For one full year he and his gang robbed stagecoaches, trains, and banks. Then the Texas Rangers set out to track him down. By the time he disappeared he was famous for stealing from the rich and giving a share of his loot to the poor.

In 1878, a lad named Shelton Story was offered a job by his neighbor, the rancher Pete Lenoir. He said he'd give Shelton a dollar to take a hindquarter from a freshly butchered cow to some friends staying in a secret place on Denton Creek. A dollar was worth a lot to Shelton, and he agreed.

"Don't ask any questions about this delivery, and don't tell anyone about it, either," said Pete.

"Pay me the dollar and I won't say a word," replied Shelton.

Shelton wrapped the beef in an old rain slicker and tied it behind his saddle. This saddle was the boy's pride and joy. He used his savings to buy it. There were fancy designs pounded into its leather, and it had elk-hide streamers and a comfortable seat. It remained new enough to creak each time he climbed on.

After an easy ride, Shelton found four hungry men hiding out in the secret camp Lenoir had sent him to. They all wore six-shooters and carried rifles. Each looked at the boy with suspicion.

"I've come to deliver beef," Shelton said nervously. "It's freshly slaughtered."

The meanest-looking of the bunch drew his gun and asked, "Who sent you?"

"Pete Lenoir. He's my neighbor."

The gunman laughed and holstered his pistol. "Why didn't you say so, kid? Get down off that horse and rest yourself. You're among friends."

Shelton dismounted and untied the hindquarter. The men were glad to have it and added big branches to the cook-fire to prepare for roasting.

The gang leader nodded at Shelton's saddle, saying, "That's a mighty fine piece of leather you rode in on, boy. How long have you had it?"

"Just a week. It's my first new-bought saddle. It's hardly broke in."

"Comfortable ride, is it?"

"Oh, yes sir, the best I ever had," Shelton answered proudly.

"I have an idea, boy. You see that rig on the ground?" He pointed to an old, worn-out saddle. It wasn't worth more than a few dollars.

"Yes."

"I want to make a trade with you. My saddle for yours."

Shelton gulped. The three other men reached for their rifles. The leader rested his hand on his pistol-butt. With a lump in his throat and a pain in his heart the boy shook his head. "Okay."

The saddles were exchanged. With downcast eyes, Shelton adjusted the old rig's stirrups and swung up onto his horse.

"Do you know who you've been trading with, lad?" asked the leader.

"No, I reckon I don't."

"Sam Bass. And now you best be heading back. And not a word about who got your saddle."

Shelton rode home feeling bad. Sam Bass had turned out to be just another low-down crook. The old saddle he had gotten was made of good leather, and it had well-worn saddlebags attached. But he hated it. As soon as he got home he would throw it away.

After reaching his dad's barn, Shelton got down from the horse and loosened the saddle. It slipped out of his hands and hit the ground. Something went *clink*.

He opened one of the saddlebags and dug out three twenty-dollar gold pieces. Then he found three more of them in the other bag. He whooped and hollered with joy!

The next morning, Shelton went to town and bought the finest rig in the state of Texas. He started with a Navajo blanket, added a new saddle with silver trimmings, and used the rest of his money to buy a pair of fancy boots with silver spurs.

It wasn't long afterward that Sam Bass was gunned down by the Texas Rangers. Shelton Story wasn't the only one to shed a tear for the Robin Hood of Texas.

The Haint that Roared

ALABAMA

Long ago, in the backwoods of Alabama, a wealthy merchant built a beautiful house with many rooms. He lived there in happiness for many years. Then one night, something horrible happened.

Thieves had heard that the merchant kept a chest of gold hidden somewhere in the house. They were determined to have it. After waiting until the moon became a thin crescent of light, they sneaked into the merchant's bedroom and demanded he give up the gold.

"Never!" he yelled. "It's mine, and I'll keep it throughout eternity."

He was tortured and finally killed, but true to the merchant's words, the gold remained hidden. The thieves were so angry that they cut his body into parts out of spite.

For many years afterward his big house remained

boarded up. But when the moon became crescent, strange cries could be heard coming from inside. The neighbors were sure the house was haunted.

Then one day a brave lad walked up to the house. It was raining hard, and he needed shelter. He pried the boards loose from a first floor window and climbed in.

After exploring several dusty rooms, he started a fire in the fireplace. He filled a big black pot with water to make himself a stew with vegetables plucked from the abandoned garden. Then he wrapped himself in a moldy blanket and waited for it to be done. It grew dark. The only light came from the fireplace.

Suddenly, from up in the brick chimney, he heard a shaking, followed by a roar. *"Down I come! Ready or not, down I come!"*

"Well, quit your hollering and come on down," yelled the lad. "And be careful. Don't fall into my stew."

To his amazement, a pair of legs with bare feet plopped right into the pot and splashed vegetables and broth onto the fire.

"Now look at what you've done," said the boy. He removed the legs from the stew and laid them on the floor.

The chimney rattled again and the voice screamed, *"Down I come! Ready or not, down I come!"*

"Quit your bellyaching and come on down," said the boy. "Just be more careful and don't fall into the pot."

Two arms fell into the stew with a loud *kersplash!*

The lad took them out of the pot and laid them on the floor, next to the legs.

The chimney shook and rattled a third time. The voice yelled, *"Down I come! Ready or not, down I come!"*

"Fall on down and see if I care," replied the boy. "Just stay out of my dinner."

A man's torso sunk into the pot, sloshing more stew onto the fire and nearly putting it out.

The boy yanked the torso out and laid it on the floor between the arms and the legs.

Once more the chimney shook and rattled and the voice roared, *"Down I come! Ready or not, down I come!"*

"You might as well aim for the pot," said the boy. "You've already ruined my supper."

A man's head bounced down from the chimney, hit the edge of the pot, and rolled across the floor. After settling into place next to the other body parts, it squished together with the torso. Then the arms and legs moved into place. Soon a full-bodied man sat up and looked the boy over.

The boy looked back. "You look starved." He held out his spoon. "How about some stew? You're the only one to touch it, and I'll bet it's tasty."

The man shook his head, still looking the boy over.

The boy held his gaze. "You look cold." He slipped the blanket off his shoulders, saying, "It's going to be chilly tonight. Why don't you wrap up in this blanket? I'll bet I can find another in this big old house."

The man shook his head. His eyes remained on the boy.

The boy blinked his eyes. This man was dead!

"You've got good manners, boy," said the ghost. "Most folks think I'm a mean old haint and run away. You're the first to stay and be civil."

"Why do you hang around this big ol' house?"

"I swore to watch over my gold. It's been buried

down in my basement for fifty years. Now I want you to have it. Then I can leave this place and rest in peace."

The haint showed the lad where to dig, and sure enough, the chest was still there. The haint drifted back up the chimney and disappeared, never to be heard from again.

Now that the youth was rich, he fixed up the big house and married a fine woman. They had lots of children. When the kids misbehaved at bedtime, he would rattle the chimney and roar, *"Down I come! Ready or not, down I come!"*

Jack and the Bogey Man

TEXAS

Jack was a happy lad, but selfish. It was the custom in Texas to share fresh meat with one's neighbors, but Jack wouldn't do it. Whenever he butchered a hog, he ate it all himself. He didn't like his neighbors, and they didn't like him.

One day the neighbors decided to get back at Jack by sending for the Bogey Man. The Bogey Man was hideous looking. His face had been struck by lightening when he was a child, causing his mouth to be frozen nearly shut. Since he couldn't eat, he survived on milk. Because of his mouth, he had to suck it through a straw.

Whenever the Bogey Man appeared, people would run away in fright. But not Jack. He befriended old "frozen face."

At meal time he would say, "I just finished with the milking. Can I offer you a gallon or two?"

Soon the Bogey Man felt right at home. He said, "I'll move in with you permanent, Jack, if you don't mind."

"Not at all," replied Jack. "We can farm together and split the profit. We'll make a good team."

"You won't try to cheat me, will you, Jack? I'd get awful mad if you cheated me."

"Cheat you? How could I cheat anyone as big and mean and ugly as you? Let's work on a vegetable garden."

Their first crop was sweet potatoes. Soon the ground was covered with pretty green vines. When harvest time arrived, Jack asked the Bogey Man, "Do you want the half that grows on top of the ground or the half that grows beneath?"

"I'll take what I can see. I want the tops."

Jack grinned. "Then all the sweet potatoes are mine."

When the Bogey Man realized that the vines weren't worth anything, he was mighty mad. Jack said, "Don't worry. We'll grow another crop next year."

Next they planted oats. The rains were good, and the stalks grew tall. At harvest time Jack said, "OK, Bogey Man, what do you want this year, tops or bottoms?"

"I took tops last year and didn't make any money. This year I want what grows below the ground."

Jack got all the oats. The Bogey Man was left with worthless roots. He was fit to be tied.

Jack said, "Don't worry. Now we'll raise hogs and split the profits fifty-fifty."

They started with a bunch of piglets. Soon they were big and fat. A certain papa hog grew to be the biggest and strongest of all.

One day Jack said, "It's time to divide the hogs into

two bunches so that we can sell them fair and square."

The Bogey Man was two times bigger and three times stronger than Jack. He was ready to take the lead. So he said, "Let's build two separate pens, one for you and one for me. Tomorrow morning, when the clock strikes six, each man keeps all the hogs he can toss in his pen."

"Sounds good to me," said Jack.

Jack knew that the Bogey Man would grab the biggest one first. So he took a bucket of axle grease down to the pigpen late that night and greased the papa all over.

The sun came up and the clock struck six. The Bogey Man went for the papa hog, who squealed and slipped loose. Meanwhile Jack grabbed one pig after the other. Again and again, the papa hog slipped away from the Bogey Man. By the time he wrestled him into a pen, Jack had captured all the others.

The Bogey Man was boiling mad. All he had to show for three years' work was one fat pig. He told the neighbors that Jack was too smart for him, and he went away.

After that, Jack's neighbors stopped complaining about his being selfish. Instead they called him smart.

Jack liked that. Then, whenever he would butcher a hog, he would share it with his neighbors.

MIDWEST

The Midwest stretches from the hills of Appalachia to the majestic Rocky Mountains. The Great Lakes and the Missouri and Mississippi rivers create fertile land for abundant crops of corn and wheat. Sprawling plains and dry prairies support all manner of livestock. The uplands of the Dakotas were once home to dinosaurs.

My maternal grandparents scratched out a living as farmers in Coffeyville, Kansas, on the Oklahoma border, in the 1940s and '50s. As children, my brothers and I sat on the porch with Grandpa Wayne to watch storms brewing in the vast and darkening sky. He told us about killer tornadoes and how we could hide in the root cellar. Grandma Dolly cooled apple pies on the windowsill and always made us wash hands and faces before dinner. Their lives were filled with hard work and abundant love.

Midwest stories are born of work and love. The land demands commitment, and nothing comes easily. The heart has ample opportunity to choose goodness over pain. I feel at home in the Midwest. The heart of a story is usually found at home.

What Gold?

Charles H. Withington brought his wife to southern Kansas in 1853. They settled in Council Grove, and he opened the first dry goods store there.

Because there was no bank to handle his finances, Mr. Withington kept his own accounts. Gold was often used for purchases. Before long he had a sack of valuable bullion.

Charles trusted his wife more than he trusted himself. Mrs. Withington was as smart as she was brave. The heavy sack of gold was stored with her.

Charles had to leave town on business one morning, and he was worried about leaving his wife alone. The day before, a band of robbers called the Anderson Gang had been spotted in the next county. They were a group of four riders with a serious reputation for taking what they wanted.

"I don't know if I should go, dear," he said to his wife. "The trip is important for business, but the Andersons will have heard about our gold."

"What gold? There's no gold here."

Charles smiled. "Yes, dear. Whatever you say. I'll be home by dark."

It was wash day. Mrs. Withington took a big tub down from the wall and set it on two sawhorses on the front porch. After filling it with cold well water, she added a pile of dirty clothes and lots of soap. Then she pulled up her sleeves and set to work.

It wasn't long before she noticed a cloud of dust in the distance. The Anderson Gang was headed for her prairie cabin. Since she had known the Anderson family before they went bad, she showed no fear as the four men rode into her yard.

"Howdy, Mr. Anderson," she sang out. "You and your boys look thirsty. The well is on the side of the cabin. Help yourself."

Mr. Anderson touched the brim of his dusty hat. "Thank you kindly, Mrs. Withington. We are thirsty... hungry, too. I remember the Sunday you invited my family over a few years back. The meal was mighty tasty. Fix us something to eat."

"Nice of you to remember," she replied. "That was before you started robbing folks. As I recall, you were invited to supper. You didn't ride in and order up a meal. Not even my husband gets away with that. He shows me proper respect. He asks me..."

"All right, all right. I see what you're getting at. I'm asking you. Please fix us something to eat. We're mighty hungry."

"Then come on in and I'll see what I can do."

She prepared a hearty meal of cold ham and beans, fresh cornbread, and strong coffee. The men ate with gusto and offered compliments.

Finishing the last crumb of cornbread, Mr. Anderson wiped his mustache with his hand and said, "Now hand over your gold, Mrs. Withington, and we'll be on our way."

"What gold is that?"

"The gold from your husband's store. Everyone knows that you're in charge of it. Hand it over and there won't be any trouble."

"I'm sorry, Mr. Anderson, but there isn't any gold. Mr. Withington would never leave such a thing for you to steal."

"You'll excuse me if I don't believe you," he replied. "Hand it over."

"There's nothing to hand over."

"We'll search the cabin."

"I doubt I could stop you. Anyway, I must finish the washing."

Search they did, through the entire cabin. First they tossed everything out of the cupboards and bureaus. Then they cut open the mattress and shook out the pillows. After moving every piece of furniture, they pounded on the log walls. They found no gold.

Mrs. Withington remained on her porch, washing.

The men tried the top of the cabin's roof, under the porch, and even the outhouse.

Completely frustrated, Mr. Anderson pulled his pistol from the holster and pointed it directly at Mrs. Withington. "This is your last chance, lady. Tell me where the gold is hidden."

She looked him right in the eye. "You may as well pull the trigger, Mr. Anderson. There is no gold to find."

He stared at her for a moment longer, then holstered his gun. He knew he'd been stood up to. The gang rode away.

Mrs. Withington finished the washing just as her husband rode into the yard. When he got down from his horse, he hugged her tight.

"I heard on the road that the Andersons paid us a visit. Did they get the gold?"

"This gold?" She pulled the heavy sack from the bottom of the washtub, where it had laid hidden all day under soapy water and soggy clothes.

What You Wish For

OJIBWA/MICHIGAN

All-powerful Manibozho, the Trickster, had grown old and tired. To get away from the people, he built a lodge deep in the primordial forest, far across the crystal waters. Now he was content to rest. He wanted to listen to the wind's song. He yearned to warm his feet by the fire.

"People are troublesome," he said to himself. "I'm better off without them."

The name of Manibozho was already legendary in the villages. Parents told their children of his adventures, then hinted that he could work magic as well as grant wishes.

In one tribe, ten boys grew into young manhood wishing to meet Manibozho. After discovery of their shared desires, all ten agreed to band together and search for their hero.

Their journey was long and difficult. They traveled through forests too dense for trails and paddled canoes across lakes lacking names. Again and again they confronted challenges and kept going. Finally, after seven full moons, they stumbled upon the hidden dwelling place of Manibozho.

He sighed, then invited them in. All ten crowded into his lodge and sat around his fire.

"Why have you tracked me down?" asked the old trickster.

"Because of your great powers," said the first young man. "We did a lot of talking on the trail. Each of us has a secret wish. We're hoping that you will make it come true."

"If I give you what you wish for, will you go and leave me in peace?"

"Yes," said the second youth, "we will go."

"All of you?" asked Manibozho.

Each one nodded.

"Very well. Then we will do this one at a time. Tell me what you most desire and I'll make it happen. But be certain that what you wish for is what you truly want."

The first youth said, "I want to be a great warrior."

"So you will," said Manibozho. "You'll be victorious in battle and all men will fear your strength. You'll become a powerful chief, and your name will be remembered long after you die."

A second young man said, "I love the art of healing. I wish to be the best possible man of medicine."

"I grant your wish," said the Trickster. "You will get to know the healing herbs and learn how to interpret dreams. You will master the words and the rhythms of healing chants. Great Spirit will whisper into your ear and allow you to tell the people what they are ready to hear."

A third seeker said, "I want to become the most skillful hunter of the tribe."

"You may have what you wish for," said the giver of gifts. "Your eyesight will be keen and your aim steady. You will track your prey without making a sound or leaving a scent. You will bring home meat and skins for the people. They will praise you in story and song."

And so it went. The fourth youth asked for wealth. The fifth desired the beautiful daughter of a chief. The sixth wanted to chip the finest arrowheads. The seventh yearned for ten sons of his own. The eighth longed for skill with horses. The ninth simply wanted to become handsome.

Manibozho granted each his wish.

Then the tenth youth said, "I want to live forever."

Trickster looked at him long and hard. "Is this your true desire?"

"It is."

"I have agreed to make each of your wishes come true. I must keep my word. Eternal life is yours."

So saying, Manibozho changed the youth into a big rock. Winter winds and summer sun, years building upon years, and the forces of nature do not weaken, do not kill such a man. Eternity is his.

The rock rests on Mackinac Island on the northern rim of Lake Huron. Today it's known as Sugar Loaf Rock.

Saint Johnny of the Apple Orchards

OHIO

He wore a cooking pot for a hat and carried a sack full of apple seeds over his shoulder. He had an old Bible in his pocket and hated to wear shoes. His name was John Chapman, and he was the man who brought apples to the American frontier.

Born in Leominster, Massachusetts, in 1774, Johnny Appleseed, as he came to be called, began his odyssey at the age of twenty-three. Traveling west through Pennsylvania, Ohio, and Indiana, he planted seeds and cultivated orchards wherever he went. A devout Christian, he became a follower of the Swedish philosopher Emanuel Swedenborg, who preached that the road to heaven lay in simple harmony with nature. His admirers called him "Saint Johnny."

A broken engagement had shattered his heart when he

was a young man. Not until he turned to God and found his mission did he blossom anew. Along with apple seeds and Bible quotations—which he called "fresh news from heaven"—he offered verses from his own poems.

> I sing my heart into the air,
> And plant my way with seed,
> The song sends music everywhere,
> The tree will tell my deed.

In 1801, Saint Johnny arrived in the Ohio Territory. Hungry bears lurked in its primeval forests. Timberwolves occupied its rocky valleys. Rattlesnakes ruled the land. Johnny rode, walked, and camped without fear. Wherever he went he chose to celebrate beauty.

Since he was traveling alone, he graciously accepted offers of a meal and a place to sleep whenever they were offered. Unless it was freezing cold, he ate his food on the porch so that he could share it with the birds and the squirrels. He loved to tie a hammock between stout tree branches and sleep beneath the stars.

When asked where he lived, he'd answer, "Nature is my home. The earth is my floor, and the sky is my roof. I've made friends with the sun and the wind and the rain. Nature is also my teacher. The more I learn, the less I need. The less I need, the happier I am."

The Indians respected Johnny and welcomed him to pass through their lands. They considered him a holy man because of his love of nature and indifference to pain.

Because he went barefoot in all kinds of weather, the soles of his feet grew coarse and thick. One day a rattlesnake bit him in the foot and still he didn't complain.

One of his friends wanted to kill the snake, but Johnny said, "No. It's all part of the game."

On one winter journey, he walked through a virgin forest without cabins for shelter. At nightfall he came upon a large hollow log. When he started to crawl inside, he heard a soft grunt. A hibernating mother bear had already claimed that spot. Johnny backed out saying, "Sorry, Sister Bear. I didn't realize I was intruding." He made a shelter of branches and snow and slept in the cold.

After rescuing a full-grown wolf from a hunter's steel trap, Johnny acquired a traveling companion. The gray wolf stayed with him for years. Then one day a hunter mistook the wolf for wild and shot him. It was one of the few times that Johnny was seen in tears.

As he grew older, his appearance grew even stranger. He changed his headgear from tin pot to pasteboard hat with a large bill to protect his eyes from the bright sun. He traded his ragged coat for a gunnysack with holes for his arms and legs. He didn't trim his beard, and he let his hair grow long.

His manner kept pace with his looks. He began to talk with animals and trees, and he seemed radiantly blissful wherever he went.

Children were drawn to Johnny, and he loved them in return. He would arrive with a piece of calico cloth for the girls and some string or a piece of carving wood for the boys. And he would speak to them as equals.

Parents had good reason to appreciate Johnny as well. When he heard about trouble, he would travel day and night to warn settlers of impending raids. He saved many lives.

Late in his life, Johnny traveled from Ohio to Indiana to create a new belt of apple orchards. In 1845, he arrived at a friend's cabin near Fort Wayne. Now seventy-two, he ate a final meal on the porch and watched the sun set in the west. Then he lay down by the fire, went to sleep, and didn't awake. Carved on a stone in Ashland, Ohio, is this simple epitaph:

Johnny Appleseed
Patron saint of American orchards
Soldier of peace
He went about doing good.

Calamity Jane

SOUTH DAKOTA

The gold rush of 1876 brought hoards of prospectors to Deadwood, South Dakota. Martha Jane Canary came with them. She was born at a Wyoming trading post in 1860. Two years later, Sioux warriors killed her parents. Martha Jane was taken to Fort Laramie and raised by an army sergeant and his wife. Even as a child she ran wild. That's when folks started calling her Calamity Jane.

Calamity learned to ride, shoot, hunt, and, when necessary, fight. She dressed in buckskins, chewed tobacco, drank hard liquor, and never backed down from a man. She delivered mail with the Pony Express until she was recruited as a scout for General George Custer. Married twice, she said that the only man she ever truly loved, but didn't marry, was Wild Bill Hickok.

Calamity put her extraordinary energy to work for

good as well as trouble. Few nurses and even fewer doctors were available when the smallpox epidemic hit Deadwood in 1878. Those infected usually died within a month. Those who tried to help often ended up sick, too.

One time when six men were down with smallpox in Deadwood, word was sent for Dr. Babcock to come. By the time he arrived, the men had been quarantined in a small log cabin.

Calamity met him at the door. "It's about time you showed up," she said. "These men are too weak to get a drink of water."

Dr. Babcock's voice was full of concern. "You'll probably get the smallpox if you stay."

Calamity remained cool. "No one else is willing to help. Tell me what to do for them."

She nursed the men through several painful weeks. Two died. Four survived. She herself remained well.

Then there was the time a boy in Deadwood came down with mountain fever. Close to dying, he asked for a big sour pickle. The doctor said that it would kill him. The boy insisted.

Calamity brought him the pickle. "If it's going to do him in, I'm responsible," she said. "So I guess I'll have to stay and care for him."

Years later, the boy grown to manhood remembered, "I owe my life to Calamity. And that sour pickle!"

Calamity Jane loved the excitement of an adventure. When Wild Bill Hickok asked her to be in his Wild West Show, she didn't hesitate. She even made it to the Pan-American Exposition in Buffalo, New York.

As a betting woman, Calamity devised one of the

craziest horse races ever run. One afternoon while she was sitting on the porch of a saloon, a stranger rode up. He admired her horse, whose name was Jim, but said that his own horse was faster.

"Are you willing to wager on that bold brag?" she asked.

"I'll bet you one hundred dollars that my horse can outrun your Jim anytime, anywhere, and anyhow."

"Stranger," she smiled, "if I get to set all the conditions of the race, you have a bet."

He agreed. Both of them gave a hundred dollars in cash to the sheriff to hold, winner take all. Then Calamity explained how the race would be run.

"We'll begin at the far end of Main Street and race to this saloon. The horses will have to jump up onto the sidewalk, walk through the swinging doors, and up to the bar. We'll each have a drink and ride back out to the street. Then we'll head down to the next saloon and do the same thing. There are eleven saloons in this town. The first horse to sidle up to the eleventh bar wins."

The stranger didn't realize that Jim had been trained to carry her into saloons. He could even pick up a bottle with his teeth and drink from it. This trick had been winning them both free drinks for years. Calamity won the race by four saloons and five drinks.

When she was fifty years old, Calamity Jane died in a miner's camp in the mountains above Deadwood. Her funeral was held in the town's small Methodist church. Every seat was occupied. The minister spoke of Calamity's virtues. He made no mention of her faults. She had told her friends that she wanted to be buried next to Wild Bill Hickok. And so she was.

One day a stranger was spied sitting beside her grave, sobbing away. When asked how he knew Calamity, he replied, "I was her first husband. She was the kindest woman who ever lived."

Jesse James Saves the Day

MISSOURI

The outlaw brothers Jesse and Frank James liked to hide from the law in the Ozark Hills. One afternoon they rode up to a small cabin and asked the woman at the door for a meal.

"We'll pay handsomely," said Jesse.

The woman wiped a tear from her cheek and said, "I haven't got much, but you're welcome to what I have."

Jesse noted the general air of sadness and tipped his hat, saying, "My brother and I are sorry for your troubles, Ma'am."

"Nothing you can do about 'em," she whispered. "Might as well get a cool drink from the well and sit on the porch for a spell. It'll take time to cook a chicken."

"Thank you kindly, Missus," said Frank.

As she prepared the meal, the outlaws walked about her small farm. The tumbledown barn housed three thin cows. The vegetable garden was picked nearly clean. The James brothers were sure she wouldn't last much longer on the land.

"Let's see what's up," said Jesse.

"Let it be, brother," replied Frank. "You can't always be sticking your nose into other folks' affairs."

"Can too," said Jesse with a grin.

When the meal was ready, the woman asked them to come inside. Jesse saw that the table held two place settings.

"Join us for supper, Ma'am. We'd like your company."

"No, I can't eat. I have too much on my mind."

"Sometimes it helps to talk. That's what my maw always says. My brother says I talk too much, but that's my way. Get yourself a plate and pull up a chair."

It didn't take long for the three hungry people to devour this meal of roasted chicken, boiled potatoes, and hot corn bread dripping with butter.

Jesse wiped his mouth. "You're a fine cook, Missus. If you have to leave this farm, you can always hire on as a roadhouse cook."

His words burst an emotional dam. She put her head down on the table and began to sob.

Jesse patted her on the shoulder. "Tell us about it."

She regained control and her story poured out. "Just last month my husband died. He was cutting timber and a tree fell the wrong way. It landed on top of him.

"A week after he was buried, Mr. Grady, the banker, came to my door. He showed me the mortgage papers on this farm. Said that I couldn't run it by myself and I'd better pack up and leave. Said I had to pay everything owed or he'd take it over by tomorrow morning!"

"How much is owed?" asked Frank.

"Four hundred and eighty dollars. I have fifty at most. What can I do?"

"Do you want to stay?" asked Jesse.

"Yes, I want to stay. My husband and I worked ten years to make this land our home."

Jesse glanced at Frank and smiled. Frank looked at Jesse and nodded.

"We'll make you a loan! We have just enough cash to pay off your mortgage. You can pay us back when you have it."

"But it might take me years to pay you back."

"Not with the way you cook. People will pay for that. Every now and again we'll stop by to see how you're doing. Sound okay?"

"Are you sure?"

"Let's get down to business," said Jesse. "I'll get the money from my saddlebags. Frank will look over your mortgage papers. When this Grady fellow shows up tomorrow, make sure you get a signed receipt for the cash."

"And make sure he signs the mortgage over to you as paid in full," said Frank.

"I'll be sure," she said, now weeping with gratitude.

Jesse and Frank saddled their horses. Before riding away they asked, "What does Mr. Grady look like?"

"He's rather short. He has a withered arm. His left one."

"And what does he usually wear, Missus?" asked Frank.

"Black suit. And he likes a bow tie."

"Does he ride a horse or drive a wagon?" asked Jesse.

"Horse. A roan, if I recall."

"And what time are you expecting him tomorrow morning?" asked Frank.

"Around ten. That's what he said."

"He'll want to know where you got the money," said Frank. "Best you not say a word about us being here."

"Not a word," she replied.

The brothers touched the brims of their hats and rode away.

The banker rode into her yard an hour early the following morning. He was anxious to take the farm.

"The debt is due," he said, "and I'm here to collect."

"But I have the money, Mr. Grady, every penny. Come in and we'll take care of business."

Surprised and disappointed by this turn of events, the banker left with the money. It was on his ride back to town, about five miles from the farm, that two masked men with drawn pistols stopped him on the road. Upon searching him they found five hundred dollars in cash.

"Thank you kindly," said one of the bandits.

The other just laughed.

They rode away, leaving Mr. Grady a great deal poorer.

ROCKY MOUNTAIN

Rumors of riches brought legions of wagon trains across the plains to the Rockies. Miners, ranchers, gamblers, and dreamers settled new-made gold camps and Wild West towns. Cowboys grew legendary and outlaws achieved celebrity. Hero tales abounded.

My brothers and I were born and raised in Denver, the "Mile High City." My dad often said, "Boys, we live in the finest state in the union. We have it all: sunshine, mountains, clean air, and rainbow trout."

Hunting and fishing were family traditions, and our dinner plates regularly held venison, trout, and pheasant. We climbed rugged mountains and camped alongside raging rivers. We shared stories around campfires and slept under canopies of bright stars. We were among the final generation to experience the Old West. Perhaps that explains my attraction to western ghost towns.

Stories from Colorado, Montana, Wyoming, Nevada, Utah, New Mexico, and Arizona expand our nation's character, romanticize her personality, and solidify her past. I try to fit one into every storytelling program.

Buffalo Bill Cody and the Bandits

ROCKY MOUNTAINS

William F. Cody was born in 1846 on a farm in Scott County, Iowa. By the time he reached twenty-three, he was skilled as a hunter and army scout. When he turned twenty-six, he was hired by the Kansas Pacific Railroad to supply buffalo meat to its construction crews. Soon he was called Buffalo Bill. His reputation as a rifleman and risk-taker made him famous throughout the west.

In the Old West, bandits were called road agents. During the summer of 1866, they robbed several pony express riders. After one rider was killed during a holdup, Cody was asked to deliver the rider's mail pouch. It contained important letters and a valuable payroll.

Young Buffalo Bill realized that he faced a difficult challenge. While riding to a relay station, he thought about his options. Bandits could be hiding somewhere on the trail to the next station. Since they knew he was carrying a payroll, an encounter seemed likely.

Determined to protect his cargo, Cody came up with a plan. He placed the saddlebags holding the valuables in front of his saddle and covered them with a horse-blanket. Then he filled a second pair of saddlebags with worthless papers and lay them over the blanket hiding the first pouches.

After checking to see that his revolver was loaded, Cody began his dangerous journey. When he entered a desolate valley several miles up the road, he realized it was an ideal place for a holdup. He slowed down so that he could remain alert.

Suddenly two masked men jumped from behind thick shrubs. Their rifles were aimed at his head and his heart. The tallest man's words brought him to an abrupt halt.

"Pull up or die, Bill Cody. We know you're carrying a payroll."

"I intend to deliver it," he said in response. "You'll hang if you steal it."

"We'll take our chances," said the second outlaw. "Throw down those pouches."

"There's nothing of value in them," said Bill.

"We want them anyway," replied the first man. "Give up the mail or die. You decide."

Cody shook his head as he began unfastening the saddlebags. "Mark my words, both of you. This will bring you misery."

"Let us worry about that," said the second bandit.

Raising the bags high with one hand, Cody whipped his revolver out with the other, yelling, "Take them!" He hurled the bags past the tall man's head. The robber turned to see where they landed. Cody shot the second man in his arm. The tall man swung back around, but it was too late. Cody spurred his horse, and the horse knocked him to the ground.

As the pony-rider galloped away, leaving the road

agents in the dust, he yelled triumphantly. The tall man fired two shots at him, but both of them missed.

When he arrived at the next station on time, Buffalo Bill Cody was commended by one and all for saving the payroll.

His prophecy regarding the bandits came true. The following year, both of them were caught and hanged.

Not Even a Saint

NEW MEXICO

Farmer Ysidro, later known as the Farmer's Saint, eked out a living by growing beans and chilies on his small farm near the Rio Grande. Following God's laws, he plowed hard ground and planted precious seeds by May 15, the day known as San Ysidro's Fiesta Day. The rains didn't fall one planting season, and Farmer Ysidro's land grew thirsty. He worried that he wouldn't get his seeds in the ground on time and would lose the next crop.

May 15 arrived with a blistering morning sun. Ysidro hitched his ox to the plow and began preparing the field. "Better late than not at all," he said to the dry wind. He worked for an hour before stopping for a drink of cool water.

Suddenly, a tall, brown-skinned angel surrounded with golden light appeared, saying, "God is unhappy with you, Ysidro. This is a holy day, a day of fiesta, a day of honor. It's a day to celebrate. God asks you to cease your labors."

Farmer Ysidro wiped his brow with a kerchief, thought for a moment, and replied, "I'm pleased that God cares about me. Tell Him that the rains are late this year and I must get my seeds in the ground today. I'm sure He will understand."

"No," said the angel, "God doesn't understand. If you refuse to lay down your plow, He will send powerful winds and heavy rains to destroy your next crop."

"Tell God that even though it's a holy day, I can't stop. If He sends a storm to harm my beans and chilies, I'll deal with it. Let me get on with my work."

The angel disappeared and Farmer Ysidro continued plowing. A second angel appeared an hour later. She was taller than the first and her golden light shown even brighter.

"God is disappointed with you, Ysidro. He insists that you rest on this holy day and participate in the fiesta. Put down the plow and leave the planting for tomorrow."

Ysidro kept driving the ox forward, digging the furrow deep as he went. "Ask God to please leave me alone on this special day," he said. "He can see that I have a lot of work ahead if I'm to get the crop planted by nightfall. Tell Him I can't stop."

"God says that if you don't obey, He will throw bolts of lightning to burn your field."

"I can't help that," replied the farmer wearily. "It's past time to plant. I have to do what I can. Ask Him to try and understand."

The angel disappeared and Farmer Ysidro continued to work and sweat under the broiling sun.

At high noon the third angel appeared. He was even taller and brighter than the first two.

"God is most displeased with you, Ysidro. He has asked you twice to stop your labors on this important day. Twice you have refused. I'm here to give you one final chance to honor His wishes. If you refuse, He has a special punishment in store for you."

"I know," said the farmer. "He will send a plague of grasshoppers to devour my crops."

"It's worse than that," replied the angel.

"Worse? How much worse?"

"He will send you a bad neighbor."

Farmer Ysidro couldn't believe what he had heard. He stopped his ox and let the plow handle fall to the ground. He caught his breath and whispered, "A bad neighbor?"

"Yes," said the angel, "an especially bad neighbor who will live on the farm adjoining yours."

"Please tell God that He's right, as always. I shouldn't be working on this holy day. I can handle foul weather and risk losing my crops to fire and insects, but a bad neighbor? Not even a saint can deal with a bad neighbor."

Devil's Tower

ARAPAHO/WYOMING

The Arapaho searched the vast plains for an abundant land on which to camp. They settled in an area rich in plant life and well populated with deer, buffalo, and antelope. They could tell that there were other tribes about. Since the Arapaho were cautious, they traveled in groups when leaving their new village.

One morning three young women went beyond the encampment to search for basket-weaving materials. Tall reeds and strong rushes grew on the riverbank.

"We'll find what we need upstream," said the first girl.

"My father warned us to stay close to camp," replied the second. "It's dangerous out here."

"Nonsense," said the third. "We have strong legs. We can run home if we are threatened."

So they walked far upstream and discovered an

untouched patch of materials and picked with pleasure.

"Wait until Mother sees the baskets I make with all this," said the first girl.

"My baskets will be strong as well as beautiful," said the second.

"I'm going to use a more difficult design," said the third.

Intent with busy hands and future dreams, they failed to notice a pack of bears ambling toward them in the distance. Suddenly the four bears stopped and sniffed the air. One of the girls glanced up and screamed. The other two saw the bears as well. All three of them began to run.

The bears trotted after them. The shrieking girls quickened their pace. The bears broke into a run. A deadly chase was on.

Great Spirit heard and saw all that was happening. He felt badly for the girls, as they couldn't possibly out-run the hungry bears. Nor did He blame the bears for following their natural instincts.

There appeared a large, black, flat-topped rock jutting up from the earth. The basket-weavers headed toward it. The bears followed. The girls reached the rock first and, hand over hand, pulled themselves up to the top. The four bears were natural climbers and stayed close behind.

Great Spirit realized that He would have to intervene if the girls were to live. He commanded the rock to grow upward. Slowly it rose into the sky.

The bears kept climbing. Great Spirit told the rock to grow taller yet. The bears climbed even higher, nearly reaching the top. The three girls huddled together to whisper final prayers.

Suddenly the bears' strength gave out and down they slid. Their sharp claws gouged deep grooves in the rock all the way to the bottom.

It took the girls a long time to climb back down to the earth. Night had fallen by the time they arrived home and told about their escape from the bears.

Far in the distance, a foreboding new tower stood tall against the dark sky. Its sides were scarred with deeply etched claw marks. The medicine man declared it a place of power made by Great Spirit.

Today it is known as Devil's Tower.

The Mountain Man
and the Grizzlies

COLORADO

Kit Carson was born in 1809. He left Missouri for the Rocky Mountains when he was sixteen. He only grew to be five feet, four inches tall, but he was strong and self-reliant. He became famous as a mountain man, scout, and soldier.

Kit was especially skilled as a marksman. Out hunting in the high Rockies one afternoon, he shot and killed a large elk. As soon as he lowered his rifle, a loud roar came from within the stand of trees directly behind him. Out charged a grizzly bear. He dropped his gun and ran for the nearest pine tree, several yards in the distance.

Glancing back, he saw that not one but *two* angry beasts were on the attack.

When he reached the tree, he swung up onto the first

tier of branches using all of his strength. One of the grizzlies swiped at his retreating feet with long, sharp claws. The other stood on hind legs and embraced the tree, ready to begin climbing.

Kit yanked his razor-sharp knife from its leather sheaf and hacked a thick branch loose from the tree. He raised the branch above his head, awaiting the coming assault.

Both bears began their climb. The first to reach him received a rude welcome. Kit jabbed her in the nose with the sharp end of his branch. She howled in pain and dropped to the ground.

The second bear kept on coming. Kit smacked his nose with the branch. The bear roared in anger but quickly retreated.

With their bruised noses, the grizzlies gazed up at their enemy, looking even more determined to devour him. Kit stared back at them, trying to size up the situation. "They're about ready to hibernate," he thought to himself, noticing how fat they were. "No wonder I was able to beat them to this tree. Had it been spring, when they were thinner and faster, I wouldn't have made it."

The bears shuffled around beneath his tree, preparing for another attack. Kit climbed into the highest branches and curled up, trying to make himself the smallest target possible. His rifle was lying on the ground, and he longed for its killing power.

The bears were ready for a second assault. Up they climbed, one after the other, each eyeing their prey. When the lead bear got within reach, Kit jabbed downward with the sharp end of his branch. She screamed with pain and crawled back down the trunk.

Now the male was in the lead. He held on with one paw, and with the other he swiped at Kit's dangling legs. Kit smacked his wet nose with the branch. The bear roared so loud that it hurt Kit's ears. He poked him again. This time he let go, hitting the ground with a solid thump.

Howling with frustration, the bears paced back and forth beneath the tree. Kit was sure that they would try again.

Some kind of signal seemed to pass between the pair. Simultaneously they stood up and gripped the tree from opposite sides. Instead of trying another climb, however, they began shaking the tree, hoping to dislodge their target. The shaking weakened the tree's hold in the rocky soil. Kit dropped his poke-stick and held on with both arms and both legs.

The she-bear smacked the tree trunk with her powerful paw once, twice, three times. It shook but didn't fall. The he-bear leaned in with all his weight. Still the tree didn't topple.

The battle was over. The bears shuffled back into the forest and disappeared.

Kit Carson waited for an hour before climbing down to the ground and reloading his rifle. For the rest of his life, he would say that of all his adventures and escapes, that day was the closest he had come to dying young.

Shoot-out in Benson

ARIZONA

Fifty miles west of Tucson, Arizona, lies a small town named Benson. It was the scene of one of the last great shoot-outs in the Old West. The date was February 27, 1907.

A wealthy young man named D.W. Silverton, Jr., traveled from Kentucky to Arizona to study mining operations. In Phoenix, he met and married a mysterious and beautiful young woman. She didn't tell him that she had another suitor, a fellow named Tracy.

Tracy was still waiting for the right moment to ask the woman to be his bride. When he heard that she had married Silverton, he flew into a rage.

The newlyweds left Phoenix for Tucson in order to set up housekeeping. The jealous Tracy began sending threatening letters to the new Mrs. Silverton.

When they discovered that Tracy was going to visit

Tucson, the Silvertons thought it best to leave town for a week. On the afternoon of February 26, they boarded a train for the mining town called Bisbee. When their train arrived in Benson, an overnight stop along the way, they decided to spend the night at the Virginia Hotel.

Tracy was following them on a freight train. When he disembarked in Benson, he had a Colt .45 under his jacket.

Early the next morning, Silverton walked to the train station to make certain that their coast was clear. Tracy was on the platform, standing beside the train bound for Bisbee. Silverton saw that there was a gun handle peeking out from Tracy's jacket.

He ran back to the hotel and asked the desk clerk for a gun. Arizona Ranger Lt. Harry Wheeler, another guest at the hotel, overheard their conversation and asked what was happening. Ranger Wheeler was known to be levelheaded and one of the fastest guns around. After hearing Silverton's story, he headed for the train station.

Upon spotting Tracy, Wheeler said, "Give up your weapon. I'm placing you under arrest."

Tracy pulled out his pistol and fired. His bullet ripped a hole into the left side of Wheeler's jacket but missed the man.

Wheeler drew his gun and fired once, twice, three, four times, advancing on Tracy with each shot. Tracy returned several bullets before crumpling to the platform. He'd been hit four times, in the neck, chest, shoulder, and hip. Blood spurted from Ranger Wheeler's left thigh.

"My gun's empty and I'm all in," hollered Tracy.

Wheeler nodded and put his smoking revolver back in its holster. Dragging his wounded leg, he approached Tracy.

It was a mistake. Tracy was lying. From his prone position he fired his last two shots, hitting the ranger in the right foot.

Wheeler fell to the ground next to his opponent. A large rock lay near his hand. He picked it up and smashed Tracy's skull.

The fight was over. The dust cleared.

A bystander heard Ranger Wheeler say to the loser, "Well, it was a great fight while it lasted, wasn't it, old man?"

"I'll get you yet," whispered the bleeding Tracy.

When Wheeler held out his hand, Tracy shook it.

Townspeople helped Wheeler back to the hotel and summoned the best doctor available. The Rangers sent him to Tombstone to recover. He eventually became Captain of the Arizona Rangers.

Tracy died on the way to the hospital in Tucson.

The married couple boarded the train for Bisbee.

And real life can be more exciting than fiction.

La Escalara Famosa
(The Famous Stair)

La Villa Real de la Santa Fe de San Francisco de Assisi was founded in 1610. Today it's known as the city of Santa Fe, New Mexico.

In the fall of 1852, the Sisters of Loretto left Kentucky for a hazardous journey to the Southwest. Their mission was to establish a convent in Santa Fe under the direction of Bishop Lamy.

The good bishop had hired French architect Antoine Mouly to design and build a Gothic chapel for their convent. He asked that it be a small replica of the Sainte-Chapelle in Paris, only twenty-five feet wide by seventy-five feet long and eighty-five feet in height. There was to be a small choir loft in the rear of the chapel.

The plan was slow to materialize. Soon after construction began in 1873, Antoine Mouly went blind. His son Projectus took over. Soon afterward, Projectus was shot and killed.

Skilled craftsmen were imported from Italy to complete the work. Five years later, the classically beautiful Loretto Chapel was finished. The total cost was thirty thousand dollars.

There was only one problem. A staircase leading from the floor of the chapel up to the choir loft had been overlooked. Nor was there room for one.

Local architects and carpenters were asked for advice. Their responses were remarkably similar: "Use a tall ladder, or tear the balcony out and rebuild it with a staircase."

But a change in design would have destroyed the chapel's perfect symmetry. A tall ladder would make the balcony inaccessible to all but a few of the younger sisters.

"We need the help of a true carpenter," said Magdalene, the Mother Superior. "We'll pray to Saint Joseph, sisters."

And pray they did. Their novena lasted the required nine days.

Soon afterward, an old man arrived on a burro. His hair was white. His face was deeply lined. His hands were heavily callused. He asked for the Mother Superior and, with a gentle voice, explained that he was a carpenter looking for a bit of work. She liked his quiet dignity but noted that his wooden toolbox contained only three items, a handsaw, hammer, and T-square.

When she took him into the chapel, he immediately saw the problem.

"I will build the staircase you need."

First he ordered large tubs of water to be brought in for the softening and bending of hard woods. Then he worked slowly but methodically, saying little and often humming.

His narrow staircase took on a spiral shape. It made a complete 360-degree turn by the time it was halfway to the loft. A second 360-degree turn completed the climb.

It was anchored to the floor at the bottom and solidly attached to the loft at the top, but it had no center support. Nor did this carpenter use screws or nails. His spiral stair was held together entirely with wooden pegs.

Thirty-three steps, each representing a year in the life of Jesus, arose from the floor to the loft. A double helix—two complete turns—and his work was complete. The sisters present during the construction swore that he used no more than his three tools, the handsaw, hammer, and T-square.

He arrived without wood for the project and he bought nothing from the local lumberyard. The hardwoods in his staircase are not native to New Mexico. How he got them remains a mystery.

Mother Magdalene tried to pay him several times.

"It isn't necessary" was his response.

When the staircase was completed, the Sisters of Loretto gathered in the chapel to offer prayers of thanks. When they went to say farewell to the old carpenter, they discovered that he and his burro had slipped away. He was never seen again.

"It was Saint Joseph himself," said Mother Magdalene.

Today, more than one hundred years later, the wondrous staircase is still in use. Architects and builders from around the world come to Santa Fe to inspect the famous stair. No one has been able to explain exactly how the masterpiece was constructed.

PACIFIC COAST

Idaho, Washington, Oregon, California, Alaska, and Hawaii make up the Pacific Coast region. Mountain ranges, island chains, vast deserts, and fertile valleys dominate the landscape. These are the states of extreme ruggedness, weather, and beauty. These are the states of possibility.

I honed my skills with story for twenty-six years in the Pacific Northwest. Storytelling was an unusual career choice in the early 1970s. When I explained what I did for a living, people responded with interest. "Tell me more..." was a common response. When I approached local television station directors with a fresh concept in "activating imaginations on the other side of the tube," they listened rather than scoffed. Creative attitudes prevail in the "Final Frontier." Is it any wonder that the worldwide electronic revolution is based here?

Pacific Coast stories are earthy, human, and bold. Risk is undertaken and heroes are made. Spirit looms large and anything is possible.

Scarface

Long ago, when peace ruled among tribes, a beautiful young woman refused many offers of marriage from the young men in her village.

"I cannot," she said.

"I would like to, but it isn't right," she apologized.

"You will make a good husband, but not for me," she explained.

She turned them all away because of a secret. Not even her mother and father knew the truth of it.

Years before, the Above Person, also called the Sun, had come to her. He said, "You belong to me. You must not marry an ordinary man. I will see that you live long and well. Trust what I say."

Then one day an orphaned warrior, the poorest man in the village, decided to propose to the woman. His moccasins were old and worn. His clothes were tattered. He had no horse. The only unique thing he owned was a jagged scar down one cheek.

"You turn the young men of our village away, even those who are rich, strong, and handsome. I have nothing to offer but my love. But it is true love that will last forever. Will you be my wife?"

She was deeply affected. "You speak with a kind heart," she replied. "You make me want to say yes. But I cannot.

"I will tell you my secret. The Above Person has claimed me. Go to him and ask for my release. If he agrees, ask him to remove the scar from your face. Then I will know that he approves."

Early the next morning Scarface left on his journey. He walked through the forest for days, surviving on roots, berries, and small game.

Late one afternoon he met a friendly wolf. "I seek the lodge of the Sun," said Scarface. "Can you point the way?"

"I know the forest well," Wolf explained, "but never have I seen the home of the Sun. Ask Bear."

Three days later Scarface encountered Bear. "I search for the Sun," he said. "Can you help me find the path?"

"His lodge is well hidden," answered Bear. "Only a few know the way. Perhaps Badger can help."

Scarface found Badger down his hole. "Help me, friend!" he shouted. "Help me find the lodge of the Sun."

Badger poked his striped head out of the hole. He said, "Wolverine can tell you which path is correct."

Knowing that Wolverine would be hard to find, Scarface sat on a log and cried aloud, "Wolverine is the most clever of all animals. Only he can help me. Come to me, Wolverine."

It wasn't long before Wolverine arrived. "The others have told me of your quest. The Sun's lodge lies beyond the great water. I'll point out the trail."

Scarface was grateful. He followed Wolverine on a hidden pathway to the shore of an enormous body of water. "I cannot see the other side," he exclaimed. "How will I cross such a water?"

Two swans swam up to him and said, "Climb on our backs. We will fly you across."

He placed an arm around each of the swans, and they flew him over the great water. After landing on the other side, high in sky-country, they pointed to a trail leading to the lodge of the Sun.

Scarface set out on it. He didn't stop until he came upon a strong bow with a quiver full of arrows leaning against a tree trunk. Soon afterward he saw a handsome young man approach.

"Did you see my weapons by the tree?"

"Yes," said Scarface.

"Why didn't you pick them up?"

"Because they didn't belong to me."

"Good. You are an honest man," said the youth. "And why are you in this forest?"

"I seek the Sun."

"He is my father," said the lad. "I'm Morning Star. My mother is Moon. Come, I'll take you to our lodge."

Moon greeted Scarface with kindness. "My son must trust you to bring you to our home. Why have you come?"

"Sun claims the one I love. I seek permission to marry her."

"Don't ask right away," said Moon. "Let my husband get to know you first."

Upon returning home, Sun welcomed Scarface to their lodge.

"You will be our guest," he said. "Morning Star needs a companion. You two will be good friends."

Moon took Scarface aside the following morning. "Go with Morning Star in any direction but west. West leads to the big water. There is danger there because of the geese. They have killed many of my children with their sharp beaks. Keep my son away from the geese."

Morning Star and Scarface hunted small game in the forest. Then they cooled off with a dip in the lake.

"Now let's go hunt the wild geese," said Morning Star.

"No," replied Scarface. "That might be dangerous."

Morning Star laughed and took off. He was running toward the west.

Scarface jumped up and ran after him. He arrived at the shore of the great water in time to see seven large geese attacking Morning Star. Using his spear and a club, Scarface killed all seven of them. Morning Star was scratched but not hurt. They returned to the lodge.

Sun heard the story that night and was pleased. "What can I do for you in return?" he asked Scarface.

"I wish to marry a girl of my village, the one that you have claimed for yourself. She wants me for her husband, but will not dishonor you."

"I know who you mean. She is pure of heart and strong in spirit. I give you the permission you seek."

"I thank you, Sun."

"For a wedding gift, I'll tell you how to make a medicine lodge."

So saying, he touched the youth's face and the jagged scar disappeared. Instructions for the medicine lodge were given the following day.

Now was time for Scarface to return to the earth. Moon dressed him in fine buckskin. Morning Star gave him his bow and arrows. Both led him to the Wolf Road, also called the Milky Way. It didn't take Scarface long to walk back down to the earth.

He ran to his village and found his love. She saw at once that he had lost his scar. When they were married, the feasting and dancing lasted for many days and nights. The first medicine lodge was built to honor the Sun, and the happy couple lived long and well.

His Mother Tongue

California was a province of Mexico in the early 1800s. Pedro Carrillo, a twelve-year-old boy of the Spanish aristocracy, was sent from Santa Barbara to Boston for his education. Pedro left home a boy. Six years later, he returned as a sophisticated young man.

His mother, Señora de Carrillo, was filled with joy. Her heart had known emptiness from the day he departed. Now it felt full once again. Her son had become a tall and handsome nobleman. She was very proud of him.

"Hello, Mother," Pedro said in perfect English, clicking his heels as he bowed from the waist.

He held his hand out to hers. Though surprised by his formality, she let him bestow a kiss upon it.

"The years have treated you very well," he said in formal English with a clipped Boston accent.

The Señora, desiring to show how much she approved, replied in English, "You have become a gentleman."

"Yes, but of course, Mother. And how, pray tell, are my esteemed father and younger siblings?" He was showing off his command of the second language.

Señora de Carrillo was unfamiliar with some of his words. She didn't like his superior tone of voice. This didn't seem like the boy she had birthed, suckled, and bathed.

Taking him by the arm, she escorted Pedro to the veranda and sat next to him on a leather sofa.

"Let's begin again," she said in Castilian, the boy's native language.

"But Mother mine," he replied in English, "I'm much too educated to converse the old way. Let me teach you how to speak properly."

It was all too much. The Señora got up and walked her son toward the barn. "There is something I'd like to show you, Pedro," she said.

"How delightful, Mother. A gift perhaps? A horse or a silver saddle? Yes, I could do with a silver saddle. Please don't tell me. Let it be a surprise. I love a surprise."

"I'm pleased, my son."

Once inside the barn, she closed the door and led to him to the nearest empty horse stall. From its wall she took a short-handled riding-whip with a braided leather lash. With it she struck her palm once, twice, three times.

"It seems, Pedro, that you have forgotten your mother tongue. You spoke it so well when you left home. Let me help you remember…"

Smack! Down came the whip on his shoulder. *Whack!* She struck him across his back. *Crack!* She hit his outstretched hands.

"Por favor, Mamacita! Por favor, no! Por favor!" he yelled in a torrent of Spanish. Gone was his formal Boston accent.

Pedro apologized to his mother. From that day forward he used his native language while at home—even when he went on to practice law and became a judge in the California courts.

Pu-nia and the Shark King

HAWAII

Pu-nia lived with his mother near a high cliff overlooking the clear blue sea. His father had been killed by Kai-ale-ale, the Shark King, while diving for lobsters the year before. Kai-ale-ale had ten more sharks at his command. He would allow no one to steal lobsters from his underwater cave.

Pu-nia and his mother had eaten nothing but vegetables since his father's untimely death. Now they were hungry for lobsters.

"How good a fat lobster would taste with tomorrow's meal," said his mother. "But it's too dangerous to get one. If you try, Shark King will eat you, just as he ate your father."

"Then I must outwit Kai-ale-ale, Mother."

Pu-nia knew that Shark King and his ten guards liked to nap each afternoon near the entrance of the cave.

Standing high on the cliff side, he peered down into the crystal blue water and said, loud enough for the sharks to hear, "It's good that Shark King sleeps so soundly."

Kai-ale-ale immediately woke up. But he pretended to sleep in order to hear what the boy had to say.

Pu-nia saw the huge shark open his eyes and knew that he was listening.

"I'll dive in over there on my right and steal two lobsters from under his nose."

The Shark King whispered to his ten guardians, "Devour him as soon as he hits the water."

Pu-nia tossed a heavy stone far to his right. When it splashed into the sea, all eleven of the sharks headed for it.

Pu-nia dove in and snatched a lobster with each hand. Then he swam for the cliff and climbed up onto a large, protruding rock. Eleven angry sharks were left swimming in circles below him.

"Thank you, Kai-ale-ale," yelled the boy. "My mother and I will feast tonight. And thank you, Thin Tale, for such good advice."

Nine soldier sharks immediately circled around the tenth, the one with the thin tale.

"No, no, no," protested their target. "I didn't tell him anything…"

It did him no good. With a nod from their king, Thin Tale was attacked and killed.

The following afternoon, Pu-nia returned to the cliff with a rock in his hand. The sharks were napping as usual, but he knew that they would hear him.

"Last night's feast was a treat. Mother and I want lobster again tonight. I'll dive in over there, on the left side."

He tossed the rock far out to his left. As the sharks swam toward the big splash, he dove down to their cave and grabbed two lobsters. He made it back to the rock ledge just in time.

When the sharks returned he shouted out, "Thank you again, Kai-ale-ale, for your kindness. And a special thanks to you, Spotted Fin, for telling me where to dive."

Eight of the guardian sharks encircled Spotted Fin. "It wasn't me," he cried. But it was too late. With the approval of their king, Spotted Fin was destroyed.

Pu-nia waited three days more before tricking the sharks again. This time Big Belly was killed by the others.

And so it went. Pu-nia played the trick every few days, and each time he eliminated another shark. Now Kai-ale-ale alone guarded the entrance to his cave.

Faced with only the king, Pu-nia needed a new scheme. It took him a week to come up with one.

He needed several tools to carry it out. Most important were rubbing sticks for starting a fire, charcoal for fuel, and a three-foot pole made of hard wood. He placed everything into a shoulder bag that had been woven by his mother. Then he walked out onto the rock ledge and watched Shark King swim in lazy circles below.

As usual, Pu-nia spoke loudly enough for the shark to hear. "I'll dive right in. It makes no difference if the king bites me because my mother can nurse me back to health. But if he swallows me whole I'm in trouble."

"He's mine at last," thought Kai-ale-ale.

The moment he leaped into the sea, the Shark King

opened his cavernous mouth and sucked him in whole. But before he chewed him up with his many rows of razor-sharp teeth, Pu-nia jammed the stick between his jaws to hold his mouth open.

Then the boy slipped down into the shark's belly and rubbed the fire sticks together. Once they started to smoke, he added the charcoal and created a small fire.

Gasping in pain, the Shark King dove deep. Then he zoomed up to the surface and leapt out of the water, trying to dislodge his unwelcome guest. Nothing seemed to work. When he swam around in circles, hoping to make the boy sick, Pu-nia enjoyed the ride.

Finally the Shark King grew weak. Now he headed toward a rocky shore.

Thinking quickly, Pu-nia called out, "Oh good, he's taking me to the jagged rocks where I'll be safe. If he takes me to the beach, I'll die."

Kai-ale-ale headed toward the beach. By the time he reached the soft sand, he was too weak to turn back. Pu-nia crawled out of his mouth to safety. The Shark King closed his eyes for the final time.

From that time onward, Pu-nia and his mother dove down to the cave to catch fat lobsters whenever they wished.

Paul Bunyan Makes Progress

PACIFIC NORTHWEST

Paul Bunyan, the Hercules of lumberjacks, was born in the Maine woods. A rambunctious baby, he leveled an acre of trees while learning to crawl. On the day that he turned seven, he used his daddy's saw to harvest three square miles of standing timber before lunchtime.

"He's going to be a logger," said his dad with pride. "At the rate he's growing, he'll be the best darn lumberjack in the country. Mark my words."

A strange blue snow fell one frozen winter morning a few years later. Everything was buried under a cold blanket of bright blue! Young Paul strapped on his snowshoes to explore this new landscape. Upon hearing the cry of a lost calf, he found a tiny blue ox stuck in a snowdrift. He pulled him out and took him home.

Paul named him Babe and fed him plenty of hay. The ox grew large, right along with Paul. Full grown, Babe measured seven axe-handles between his eyes.

Paul trained Babe to help him log the Maine woods. He would pull giant trees from the forest with ease. If a crooked road made it difficult to haul logs down to the river, Paul would attach one end of a thick chain to the road and the other end to Babe. Babe pulled so hard that the road would straighten right out.

After cutting down most of the tall trees in Maine, Paul and Babe moved to Minnesota. Then they took care of the forests in Michigan and Wisconsin. When they finished their work in the great North Woods, they traveled to the Far West, ending up in Oregon and Washington.

Paul marveled at this region's two hundred-foot fir trees. Their enormous brown-bark trunks had taken five hundred years and more to grow. It was the first time he'd seen trees taller than he was. Paul showed Babe the majestic Olympic Mountain Range that led to the edge of the Pacific Ocean. He thought it wonderful that the snow-capped Cascade Mountains cut through the center of this lush region. And he was delighted by all the timberwolves, grizzly bears, and long-eared jack rabbits.

"I'm a woodsman and a logger," he said to Babe. "I'm the lumberjack of all lumberjacks! I'm as old as time, as tall as a mountain, and as powerful as an earthquake. My axe will fell these trees. My saws will cut this lumber. To progress is to build. Let's help build the great Northwest!"

Paul cleared a campsite and hired a crew to make cabins and a dining hall. He forged a steel pancake griddle that covered an acre of ground. He rounded up a herd of cows and milked them each morning to make enough tasty flapjacks to feed a thousand men. The once-quiet forest echoed with the steady roar of falling trees.

Spring arrived along with the rain—lots of it. It rained so hard that all the rivers, lakes, and streams in the Northwest rose beyond their banks and flooded the land. Paul had his crew build boats so they could sail to safety. He gathered up all the forest animals, loaded them onto Babe's back, and carried them to the top of the Cascade Mountains.

When the rains finally ceased, Paul looked down from his mountain and saw the new world below. West of the Cascades, all the way to the Pacific Ocean, lay a cool, heavily wooded, emerald-green paradise. East of the Cascades all the way to Idaho lay a hot, dry, and dust-filled land.

"This place is almost ready for all the folks who are heading west," Paul explained to Babe. "But as I see it, there is no clear distinction between Oregon and Washington. Seattle is a nice town, but she needs a harbor. She'll prosper more if we find a way to get ships in from the coast. We need those ships to carry our logs to other parts of the world."

To separate Washington from Oregon, Paul hitched a gigantic steel plough to Babe and dug the Columbia River. Then, using an enormous shovel, he began digging a deep harbor to supply Seattle with a waterfront.

While creating Puget Sound, he tossed the dirt into one pile. When the pile reached fourteen thousand feet in height, it became the largest mountain around.

"It's a mighty pretty mountain," Paul said to Babe.

"Let's call it Mount Rainier."

Paul and Babe spent the rest of their days in the Pacific Northwest. They felled trees on Mondays, Tuesdays, and Wednesdays, and played in their forest during the rest of the week.

"This land is too beautiful to work all the time," Paul Bunyan explained. "Sometimes it's best to stop and have a picnic and say thanks for such abundance."

Why Animals Have No Fire

COEUR D'ALENE/IDAHO

People had fire. They cooked meat and made stews that were good to eat. They stayed warm in their lodges at night. Fire was a great blessing.

Animals lived without fire. Meat from fresh kills rotted and made them sick. They suffered from the winter cold. Animals wanted to share in the gift of fire.

Wolf and Dog were brothers. They lived in the forest and hunted together. They shared food.

One day Wolf had an idea. "Go to the people and ask for fire," he said to Dog. "Be friendly and don't frighten them. Wag your tail and lick their hands."

"I don't like people," replied Dog. "People yell at me to go away. They hit me with rocks and beat me with sticks."

"I know," said Wolf, "but people have fire. We must go to them in order to get it."

"You go to the people," said Dog. "You ask for fire."

"People are too afraid of me," said Wolf. "They try to kill me with arrows. They would never give me their gift."

"Why will they give it to me?" asked Dog.

"Because you are smaller and less threatening. Tell the people how much you admire them. Flatter them with praise. Make them laugh with your funny stories. Then ask for a little bit of fire."

Dog agreed and trotted to the place of the people. His bark was friendly and he wagged his tail. He allowed children to pet him and call him silly names. Some played run-and-hide games with him. Others gave him scraps of cooked meat that tasted good. Still others invited him to sleep by the fire. All night long he was warm.

Dog decided to remain with the people for another day before asking for their fire.

People told Dog to stay around for several days more, maybe even longer. He was tempted by the idea.

Dog stayed for a week, then a month, then a year, then on and on. He enjoyed his new life so much that he never again returned to the forest. He forgot about asking the people for fire. He forgot all about his brother, except on the cold nights when Wolf is drawn to the warmth of the people's camp. Then Dog barks at Wolf to send him away.

Eagle Island

TLINGIT/ALASKA

Many years ago, hundreds of eagles nested in tall trees on an island near Sitka, Alaska. Soaring high above the beach, they would swoop down to feast on fat salmon. They were happy.

Then early one spring, hunters in search of fish and game discovered the island. Soon they brought their families to settle this land.

Seeing the people take so many fish from the sea made the eagles concerned. Seeing the eagles take so many fish from the sea made the people concerned. The eagles and the people continued to live together on the beautiful island, but not happily.

The people distrusted the eagles. The eagles distrusted the people. An uneasy truce was formed, but sadness spread across the land. Animals stopped reproducing and began to die out. Fish swam far away from shore and could not be caught. Birds flew to neighboring islands to build their nests.

When winter came, food was scarce. Cries of starving children could be heard in the lodges every night. The people gathered for a council meeting.

"Eagles are to blame," said one of the elders. "They cause our misery."

"Yes!" cried many in response.

A boy of fifteen years, an orphan accustomed to making his way on his own, spoke up. "It's not true. Eagles are our friends. We should honor them."

It was a bold statement. He knew that others would be suspicious.

He had loved the eagles from the time he was a child. While fishing he would offer songs of praise to his high-flying friends. In return they would drop eagle feathers at his feet. The boy never failed to give the eagles a portion of his catch, even if it was but one small salmon.

"You give eagles food that belongs to hungry children," said an elder. "We have decided to leave this unhappy place. But you, Boy Who Loves Eagles More Than People, cannot go with us. You are no longer a member of our tribe. You must survive on your own."

The people packed their belongings into canoes and paddled to a distant island. The orphan was left behind. He sat on the beach listening to ocean waves washing over jagged rocks. He watched the eagles soar on the cold currents high above and sang songs of praise to them.

An eagle feather floated down in front of him. When he looked up, there was a large salmon falling from the sky. He jumped up and caught it in his outstretched arms. Dozens of eagles screeched their approval. Soon another fat salmon tumbled through the air and landed at his feet. The boy built a small fire and prepared to eat, knowing that he would be able to survive.

Soon the island lost its sadness. The animals and the fish began to return. The orphan boy lived with abundance.

Then one day a small whale beached itself on his rocky shore. The boy sliced its blubber into strips and strung them out on racks to dry.

"If only I could share all of this with my people," he said.

Suddenly Raven appeared on a branch above him and spoke. "They have forsaken you. Are you sure you want them back?"

"I'm sure," said the boy. "My belly is full but my heart is empty. What is life without community?"

Raven caught a strip of blubber with his claws and flew to the distant island. There the people were dying of cold and starvation. He dropped the blubber onto the elder's fire. When it sizzled and popped, the people ran to the fire, hoping for something to eat.

Raven sat on a branch above the fire and spoke. "You have been foolish to hate Eagle. Only the orphan you left behind has been wise. He wants you to return and share his new abundance."

The people climbed into their canoes and headed for Eagle Island. Upon landing, they approached the boy cautiously. He laughed with a glad heart and welcomed them to feast.

The people decided to return to their old home. When the boy reached manhood, he was made an elder of the tribe. He married well and raised many children.

His family totem still stands. Eagle sits at its top.

Notes

The stories in this collection are my retellings of tales—true, tall, traditional, and anecdotal—that remain popular in the six prominent regions of the United States of America.

Motifs given (where appropriate) are from Margaret Read MacDonald's *The Storyteller's Sourcebook: A Subject, Title, and Motif-Index to Folklore Collections for Children* (Detroit: Gale/Neal-Schuman, 1982).

NORTHEAST

The Chicken-Coop Jail—Massachusetts

In 1966, I became a faculty member at the University of Massachusetts in Amherst. I rented a cottage in New Salem, sixteen miles from campus, and was fortunate to have an elderly neighbor who liked to tell stories. Harold (Hank) Johnson shared this tale with me in the fall of 1967, as we watched a family of beaver working their dam at sunset. A Massachusetts native, he described Great Barrington and Springfield in detail, and told the story of Nathan Jackson with pride. He finished by saying, "I can't swear to you that it happened just this way, but I like to think it did." And so do I.

Another version of this story is found in *Tales Our Settlers Told* by Joseph and Edith Raskin (New York: Lothrop, Lee & Shepard, 1971) 63–69.

An Amazingly Long Time—New York

Emotional conservatism runs rampant in the early stories of New England. This anecdote has survived because of its accuracy of character depiction and its innate humor. Squire Wadsworth has the best line, and in the telling, I scrunch up my face, ponder for a truly long moment, and repeat the final three sentences.

In 1967, my neighbor Hank Johnson told me a similar tale regarding a lost axe. The boy was told not to return home until he found it. It took him ten years. His father had a similar response.

Still another version is found in *Comic Metamorphoses* by Dr. W. Valantine (New York: Garrett, 1855) 176–177. This one is included in *A Treasury of New England Folklore* edited by B.A. Botkin (New York: Crown, 1947) 86.

Agnes and Henry, a Love Story—Massachusetts

This love story, which remains legendary in Massachusetts, is based on fact. Samuel Adams Drake wandered throughout New England collecting legends in the early 1800s. My version is based on Drake's writings, particularly *A Book of New England Legends and Folklore in Prose and Poetry* (Boston: Roberts Brothers, 1883).

Drake's story can also be found in *New England Legend and Folklore* edited by Samuel Chamberlain (New York: Hastings House, 1967) 97–101.

The Legend of Peter Rugg—New England

Motif E510. *Phantom travelers*. The Northeast version of this legend, which is based on the theme of the Wandering Jew, first appeared in the *New England Galaxy* by William Austin in 1824. I became acquainted with Austin's story in 1974, while researching variants on the tale of the Wandering Jew. The legend of Peter Rugg is reprinted in *New England Legends and Folklore* edited by Samuel Chamberlain (New York: Hastings House, 1967) 159–166. Another version of this story appears in *Profile of Old New England* by Lewis A. Taft (New York: Dodd, Mead, 1965) 69–174.

"The Wandering Jew" is a legend based on a poem popular in France since 1774. The wanderer goes by many names. The best known are Cartophilus, Joseph Laquedem, and Ahasuerus. A good version of this story can be found in *The World's Great Folktales* edited by James R. Foster (New York: Harper & Brothers, 1953) 244–245.

The Dutchman's Inn—Pennsylvania

Motif K100. *Deceptive bargains*. It was customary for innkeepers to offer departing guests a tankard of cider "for the road." I heard this tale while staying at a bed and breakfast in Rochester, New York, during the summer of 1996. I overheard a Canadian guest share it at breakfast with a Swedish couple researching American inns for a tourists' guidebook.

A story with an identical plot appears in *American Folklore and Legend* (New York: The Readers Digest, 1978) 28.

Pulling the Rope—Connecticut

My neighbor Hank Johnson told me this story in 1967. Being young and inexperienced, I failed to appreciate its wisdom. Since then I've survived many power struggles by remembering Samuel's solution. It's a delight to pass the wisdom on.

Other versions are found in *The Housatonic, Puritan River* by Chard Powers Smith (New York: Rinehart, 1946) 258, and in *Westerly (Rhode Island) and Its Witnesses, 1626–1876* by Frederic Denison (Providence, Rhode Island: J.A. & R.A. Reid, 1878) 142–143.

SOUTHEAST

The Ghost Dog—Virginia

Motif E521.2 *Ghost of dog*. Stories about faithful dogs are told throughout the world. My sixth grade teacher, Mr. MacDonald, loved to read aloud to his students. His favorite genres were ghost stories, tall tales, and portraits of legendary figures in the Old West. This story is one of my favorites because it reminds me of Butch, my family's faithful black Labrador retriever.

Another version is found in *Folk Stories of the South* by M.A. Jagendorf (New York: Vanguard, 1972) 310–312. He traced the story's roots to Virginia.

Sam Davis and the Hangman's Noose—Tennessee

Tennessee remains proud of Sam Davis. I learned about him while visiting the state capitol in Nashville during 1975. His bronze statue still stands tall. The complete story is found in *Tennessee Tales* by Hugh Walker (Nashville, Tennessee: Aurora, 1970) 45–50.

The Big, Smelly, Hairy Toe—North Carolina

Motif E235. *Return from dead to punish theft*. Here is the version of this story I tell to children. I still recall the first and joyous time I heard it as an elementary school student. Trying to be funny rather than frightening, I leap toward different listeners with each "You?"

In 1882, a twenty-five-year-old African-American named Dupris Knight told this story to the little girl who became Mrs. Walter McCanless at Cedar Hill, Anson County, North Carolina. Her version of it can be found in *Manuscripts of the Federal Writers' Project of the Works Progress Administration for the State of North Carolina*. It is reprinted in *A Treasury of Southern Folklore* edited by B.A. Botkin (New York: Crown, 1949) 516–517.

Still another variant appears in *Folk Stories of the South* by M.A. Jagendorf (New York: Vanguard, 1972) 180–182.

Caleb's Wild Ride—Virginia

When I was living in New Salem, Massachusetts, I made the mistake of knocking a hornet's nest from my garage rafter. Well stung and feeling foolish, I asked my neighbor Hank Johnson to help remove stingers from my back. My distress reminded him of this delightful tale, which he had heard from an aunt who was born and raised in New Hampshire. Virginia and Massachusetts also claim this story.

A variant is recorded in *The Virginia Writers' Project, 1937–42,* as told by Mrs. Berry, interviewed by Susan R. Morton in Luray, Page County, in 1942. This version is reprinted in *Virginia Folk Legends,* edited by Thomas E. Barden (Charlottesville, Virginia: University Press of Virginia, 1991) 305–307.

Another variant appears in *The Jonny-Cake Papers of "Shepherd Tom"* by Thomas R. Hazard (Boston: Printed for Subscribers, 1915) 119–122.

Poor Tail-eee-poe—Kentucky

Motif E235.4.3.2 *Man cuts off tail of critter and eats it. Creature returns repeatedly for tail.* My version of this popular tale, derived from years of telling it to school children, continues to be great fun to share, not least because the story lends itself to strong vocal and physical suggestion.

After telling it in Jonesborough, Tennessee, in 1985, an older Appalachian gentleman approached me and said, "My grandpa told me that story when I was a pup. Scared me enough to keep me out of the swamp. By the way, it was a 'painter' that got him." He explained that a "painter" was a panther, which is also called cougar, puma, mountain lion, and catamount.

I discovered the story in *Old Greasybeard: Tales from the Cumberland Gap* by Leonard Roberts (Pikeville, Kentucky: Pikeville College Press, 1980) 34–36. Roberts first heard the story from Jane Muney in Leslie County, Kentucky, in 1954. Ms. Muney heard it from her grandmother, Mrs. Sidney Farmer.

An earlier version appears in *Negro Tales from West Virginia* by John Harrington Cox (New York: *The Journal of American Folklore*, Volume XLVII, October-December, 1934) 341–342.

Old Joe and the Carpenter—North Carolina

I first heard the bare bones of this, my signature story, from an elementary-school librarian in Bellingham, Washington, back in 1977. I have simplified the plot and strengthened the ending during my many years of telling it aloud. In the past twenty years, my version has been reprinted in periodicals and anthologies more than fifty times.

Perhaps the first recorded version is found in *North Carolina Folklore*. Here it is identified as "A Job of Work" by Manly Wade Wellman, Volume III, No. 1, July 1955. In 1951, the story was told to Mr. Wellman by an old bee hunter named Green who lived near Bat Cave in Henderson County, North Carolina.

GULF STATES

Pecos Bill—Texas

Pecos Bill was born of the oral tradition, through stories told by cowboys around prairie campfires. My sixth grade teacher, Mr. MacDonald, was the one who introduced him to me. One of my early writing assignments was to compose a chapter on the life of a favorite character. I chose Pecos Bill and described how he battled with Paul Bunyan over water rights to the Rio Grande.

The original written version of this story was written by Ed "Tex" O'Reilly in *Century Magazine*, Volume 106, No. 6, October 1923, 827–833. It was reprinted in *A Treasury of American Folklore* edited by B.A. Botkin (New York: Crown, 1941) 180–185.

The Bluebonnet—Comanche/Texas

Motif A2650 *Origin of flowers*. The bluebonnet, which is shaped like a summer bonnet, is the state flower of Texas. The seeds lie dormant until the fall of each year, when they burst forth and blanket the landscape with brilliant blue.

I toured Texas in the fall of 1986 as an after-dinner speaker for the Knife and Fork Clubs of America. Seeing carpets of bluebonnets for the first time, I asked about their origins and was told this Comanche legend.

Unlike other Native American tribes, the Comanche believe in several Great Spirits rather than one. Thus my use of the plural throughout.

The story initially found its way into print in "Legends of Texas" by Mrs. Bruce Reid (The Texas Folklore Society, Volume 3, 1924) 198–200.

Another version is a picture book: *The Legend of the Bluebonnet* by Tomie DePaola (New York: G.P. Putnam's Sons, 1983).

Salting the Pudding—Alabama

Motif J1820 *Inappropriate action from misunderstanding.* My mother would use the old adage—"Too many cooks spoil the broth"—whenever she felt crowded by my brothers and me in the kitchen of our childhood home. I first heard the over-salted pudding story as a graduate student in Carbondale, Illinois, in 1965, while preparing a Thanksgiving dinner with the help of too many friends in a tiny apartment kitchen.

Many variants of this story are in print. See *Folktales of America, Volume One* by Catherine H. Ainsworth (Buffalo, New York: Clyde, 1980) 83. Also *Ghosts and Goosebumps: Ghost Stories, Tall Tales, and Superstitions from Alabama* by Jack and Olivia Solomon (Tuscaloosa, Alabama: University of Alabama Press, 1981) 161–163.

Strongest of All—Louisiana

Motif K22 *Deceptive tug-of-war.* I was introduced to this popular animal tale in elementary school.

Of African origin, it was told in Louisiana in the Creole dialect. Other Africa- and Latin American versions of it put Tortoise in the role of Rabbit. See *Louisiana Folk Tales* by Alcee Fortier (Boston: Houghton, Mifflin, 1895) 3–6. (Reprinted: New York: Kraus Reprint, 1976). Also *With a Wig, With a Wag & Other American Folk Tales* by Jean Cothran (New York: McKay, 1954, 1964) 28–31.

Sam Bass—Texas

In an after-dinner program during my tour of Texas in 1986, I happened to mention the fabled Robin Hood of Sherwood Forest. An elderly woman, who had been born and raised in Denton, came up afterward to tell me about Sam Bass, the Robin Hood of Texas.

One of the earliest and best sources of this story is found in *I'll Tell You a Tale* by J. Frank Dobie (Boston: Little, Brown, 1931)154–169. He heard it firsthand from Shelton Story of Denton County, Texas.

The Haint that Roared—Alabama

Motif Q82. *Reward for fearlessness.* During the summer of 1974, I shared stories at a youth camp in western Washington. After an hour of telling around the campfire, I asked campers for contributions. A high school lad provided this adaptation of the European variant.

The boy without fear is a universal character. My portrait of him, a story developed over years of live telling, is great fun to share with younger children. Tolerant teachers tell me that the refrain, *"Down I come! Ready or not, down I come!"* has been chanted in their hallways and classrooms for days afterward.

Another version of this story is found in *Folk Stories of the South* by M.A. Jagendorf (New York: Vanguard, 1972) 10–12.

Jack and the Bogey Man—Texas

Motif K171.1 *Deceptive crop division.* The famous and clever Jack, born of Appalachian folklore and nearly always in trouble, traveled to Texas with southern white settlers and their African-American slaves. This particular Bogey Man is Texan in origin, but he has an Appalachian cousin in the Hairy Man. I first heard the Texas variant of this popular tale in Corpus Christi during my 1986 speaking tour.

For a personal account of its origin see *T for Texas, A State Full of Folklore* (Publications of the Texas Folklore Society, No. 44, 1982) 221–223. Mrs. Patt Roach heard the story from her father, Roy W. Lawson. Mr. Lawson heard it from his older brother Virgil, in Montague County, Texas prior to 1920.

Mention of the Bogey Man is also found in *Phantoms of the Plains, Tales of West Texas Ghosts* by Docia Schultz Williams (Plano, Texas: Republic of Texas Press, 1996) 245–246.

MIDWEST

What Gold?—Kansas

Motif 1892. *Deception by hiding.* Using cleverness to outwit thieves is a universal plot line. The actual locale, names, and dates used to flesh out this version of the plot make it a memorable midwestern icon.

It triggered my roots because I was fortunate enough to have maternal grandparents who farmed in Coffeyville, Kansas (on the Oklahoma border), when I was a child. I recall picking corn from towering stalks, filling sacks with fallen acorns, and riding on the broad back of a plough horse. Clearly Kansas has always demanded hardiness and wit on the part of the farmer. For this particular tale I'm indebted to a collection called *Kansas Folklore*, edited by

S.J. Sackett and William E. Koch (Lincoln, Nebraska: University of Nebraska Press, 1961) 23–24. Their version is a reprint from *History of Emporia and Lyon County* by Laura M. French (Emporia: Emporia Gazette, 1929) 177–179.

What You Wish For—Ojibwa/Michigan

Motif A977.5 *Origin of particular rock*. Manibozho, the Ojibwa trickster, has many incarnations. He was called Iktomi by the Sioux and Wak-jon-ka-gah by the Winnebago. Other tribes referred to him as Old Man, Coyote, and Raven.

Hundreds of Native American stories feature this trickster character. He is always powerful, often boastful, sometimes wise, sometimes foolish, and always full of guile. It is said that he represents all that is good as well as all that is bad in human beings.

During the summer of 1996, I traveled ten thousand miles by car, driving from Tucson, Arizona, to New York State's Adirondack Mountains and back. There were many side trips along the way. During the two days I spent in Michigan's Hiawatha National Forest, I met a park ranger who told me this story of Sugar Loaf Rock on Mackinac Island.

Another version of it can be found in *Indian Legends of American Scenes* by Marion E. Gridley (Chicago: M.A. Donohue, 1939) 55–56.

Saint Johnny of the Apple Orchards—Ohio

The story of Johnny Appleseed, a true hero among American pioneers, contains the essential ingredients of all great legends. For in real life, John Chapman was an idealistic eccentric, unselfish in his pursuits, at one with nature, and on the side of good.

Many of the tales told about Johnny Appleseed are exaggerated or simply made up. It's difficult for the storyteller to know what to include and what to leave out. Over my many years of telling, I've tried to side with basic facts, although that doesn't mean I haven't romanticized his overall story. Legends flourish because of our romanticism.

Perhaps the first written account of Chapman's life, which came twenty-six years after he died, appeared in *Harper's New Monthly Magazine*, Volume XLIII, November 1871, No. CCLVIII, 830–836. This article is reprinted in *A Treasury of American Folklore*, by B.A. Botkin (New York: Crown, 1944) 261–270.

Today there are many stories, plays, poems, and biographies

featuring Johnny Appleseed in print. See *Life Treasury of American Folklore* by the Editors of Life (New York: Time, 1961), 113–116.

Calamity Jane—South Dakota

During my tour of the country during the summer of 1996, I spent a few days in Deadwood and discovered books and pamphlets extolling Calamity Jane's virtues while justifying her supposed faults. My sixth grade teacher had introduced me to this American original, along with Annie Oakley, Billy the Kid, Wild Bill Hickok, and Jesse James.

Three of my favorite sources are *Old Deadwood Days* by Estelline Bennett (New York: Charles Scribner's & Sons, 1935); *Calamity Jane and the Lady Wildcats* by Duncan Aikman (New York: Henry Holt, 1927) 194–206; and "Calamity's Bet" from *Pardner of the Wind* by Jack Thorp (Caldwell, Idaho: Caxton, 1945), reprinted in *Great American Folklore* by Kemp P. Battle (Doubleday, 1986) 478.

Jesse James Saves the Day—Missouri

When I stumbled upon this particular story about Jesse James, I laughed, believing it to be fiction. Over the years, however, I've discovered several recountings of this incident. Now I'm sure that it contains more than a kernel of truth. Jesse's reputation as a "good" bad-man is what makes him so American.

Another version of this story appears in *Jesse James Was My Neighbor* by Homer Croy (New York: Duell, Sloan & Pearce, 1949). It is reprinted in *The Life Treasury of American Folklore* by the Editors of Life (New York: Time, 1961) 189–190.

See also *Myths, Legends and Folktales of America* edited by David Leeming and Jake Page (New York: Oxford University Press, 1999) 150–153.

ROCKY MOUNTAIN

Buffalo Bill Cody & the Bandits—Rocky Mountains

Growing up in Colorado, I was particularly impressed by stories about Buffalo Bill Cody. He, more than others, personified the West that I identified with. At ten I wanted to be a pony express rider, not a baseball player.

This anecdote comes from a book of reminiscences written by the man himself, *The Great Salt Lake Trail* by Colonel Henry

Inman and Colonel William F. Cody (New York: Macmillan, 1898) 193–198.

Not Even a Saint—New Mexico

Between 1995 and 1999, when I lived in Tucson, Arizona, I traveled throughout the Southwest in search of good stories. This tale came to me by way of a conversation at a storytelling festival in Albuquerque, New Mexico.

After hearing several of my stories, a young married couple asked if I'd heard of San Ysidro. I had, but not the story they had to tell. I particularly like it because I have a fondness for stories depicting saints as imperfect human beings.

Other versions are found in "New Mexico Legends" by Frank G. Applegate (*Southwest Review,* Vol. 10, January 1932, No. 2) 199–201; and in *Living Legends of the Santa Fe Country* by Alice Bullock (Santa Fe, New Mexico: Sunstone Press, 1972) 47–49.

Devil's Tower—Arapaho/Wyoming

Motif: A977.5 *Origin of particular rock.* In 1906, Devil's Tower was named the first U.S. National Monument. It is an impressive geological formation located in the northeast corner of Wyoming. It was prominently featured in the 1977 movie *Close Encounters of the Third Kind.*

If you visit Devil's Tower in person, you can hear, as I did, a park ranger tell this Arapaho tale of how and why it came to be.

Another version of this story appears in *Indian Legends of American Scenes* by Marion E. Gridley (Chicago: M.A. Donohue, 1939) 119–120.

The Mountain Man and the Grizzlies—Colorado

Kit Carson was another of my boyhood heroes. My father was an avid hunter, and so our dinner table often featured deer, elk, antelope, and even bear meat. When my brothers and I accompanied him into the forest, we heard stories around the campfire. Bear stories were particular favorites.

Perhaps the first printed version of this Kit Carson story came from *The Life and Adventures of Kit Carson* by DeWitt C. Peters (New York: Clark, 1859) 82–86. It is reprinted in *Tales from the American Frontier* by Richard Erdoes (New York: Pantheon, 1991) 100–102. See also *Kit Carson's Autobiography,* edited by Milo Milton Quaife (Lincoln: University of Nebraska Press, 1935) 37-39.

Shoot-out in Benson—Arizona

In 1997, I told a series of tales I had discovered locally for Tucson's NBC television affiliate, KVOA. My telling of this tale was videotaped in Benson, within sight of the actual shoot-out.

The Arizona Historical Society supplied me with an abundance of facts, photos, and old newspaper articles.

I was also helped by *Arizona Territory, Baptism in Blood*, a collection of old newspaper articles assembled by Paul L. Allen and Peter M. Pegnam (Tucson: Tucson Citizen, 1990) 43–44.

For some general background see *The Arizona Rangers* by Joseph Miller (New York: Hastings House, 1972).

La Escalara Famosa (The Famous Stair)—
New Mexico

I first visited Santa Fe's Loretto Chapel in the summer of 1966. Having been raised in a family of carpenters, I was awestruck by the workmanship of its interior staircase. I asked several questions about its origins but received few answers.

Then in 1978, upon visiting for a second time, I found a pamphlet about the construction of this stairway. When I returned in 1993, I was lucky enough to meet and talk with the chapel manager, Richard Lindsley, who provided me with the outline of this story. I still keep a photo of the staircase near my desk to remind me of the miracles that exist in our lives.

Other sources for this story include "The Inexplicable Stairs," by Sister M. Florian, *St. Joseph Magazine,* April 1960; *Light in Yucca Land* by Sister Richard Marie Barbour (Santa Fe, New Mexico: Schifani Brothers, 1952); and "Miracle or a Wonder of Construction?" by Carl R. Albach, *Consulting Engineer Magazine,* December 1965.

PACIFIC COAST

Scarface—Blackfoot/Northern Rockies

Motif H1284.1 *Scarface.* A hero tale of the highest order, this early myth has become a living legend. The renditions of it that were first heard and recorded by Caucasians tend to Europeanize the story. As an illustration of what Swiss psychologist Carl Jung dubbed "the hero's quest," it is nearly perfect.

For my own version I'm indebted to *Blackfoot Lodge Tales* by George Bird Grinnell (New York: Charles Scribner's Sons, 1892)

93–103, as reprinted by Corner House in 1972.

Another version appears in "Mythology of the Blackfoot Indians," Anthropological Papers, American Museum of Natural History, Vol. II (1908) 61–65. See also *Indian Legends from the Northern Rockies* by Ella E. Clark (Norman, Oklahoma: University of Oklahoma Press, 1966) 242–248.

His Mother Tongue—California

My Spanish teacher shared this story with our language class in San Diego, California, back in 1983. Ten years later I discovered a variant of it in *On the Old West Coast, Being Further Reminiscences of A Ranger, Major Horace Bell* edited by Lanier Bartlett (New York: William Morrow, 1930) 118–119.

Pu-nia and the Shark King—Hawaii

Motif K341.16 *Owner's interest distracted while goods are stolen.* Early Polynesians used trickster stories to teach children about nature's challenges. One of the trickster's jobs is to demonstrate ways of surviving. Pu-nia does a marvelous job of this.

I first heard this story from a Hawaiian teller who was doing school programs in Seattle.

Other versions are found in *Legends of Hawaii* by Padraic Colum (New Haven, Connecticut: Yale University Press, 1937) 92–96. And in *Hawaiian Legends of Tricksters and Riddlers* by Vivian L. Thompson (New York: Holiday House, 1969) 23–27.

Paul Bunyan Makes Progress—Pacific Northwest

The lumberjack of all lumberjacks, Paul Bunyan is generally seen as a legendary hero of the Northeast. His reputation gained a foothold in the Northwest thanks to the large number of Swedes who migrated from the woods of Minnesota and Wisconsin to the forests of Oregon and Washington State. While living in Seattle for twenty-five years, I heard innumerable variations on the theme of adventures with Paul and Babe.

A good published source is *Paul Bunyan Goes West* by Olive Beaupre Miller (New York: Doubleday, 1939) 314–332. See also *The People, Yes* by Carl Sandburg (New York: Harcourt Brace, 1936) 97–99.

Why Animals Have No Fire—Coeur d'Alene/Idaho

Motif A2513.1.2.1 *Dog sent to steal fire by wolf.* I was introduced to this tale in 1975 while on a school tour in Spokane, Washington. The mother of two elementary school students, who was a member of the Coeur d'Alene tribe, shared it with me after my program.

This story is mentioned in *How the People Sang the Mountains Up* by Maria Leach (New York: Viking, 1967) 57. See also *An Analysis of Coeur d'Alene Myths* by Gladys Reichard (Philadelphia: American Folklore Society, 1947) 193–194, reprinted by Kraus Reprint Company in 1969.

An African-American variant of this story appears in *The Favorite Uncle Remus* by Joel Chandler Harris (Boston: Houghton Mifflin, 1948) 272–277.

Eagle Island—Tlingit/Alaska

Motif B350. *Grateful animals*. Thanks to the Arts Commission of Fairbanks, Alaska, I was in residence during an exceptionally cold week in February 1978. I met a Tlingit husband and wife who told me this story and other Tlingit legends after an evening library program.

Another version can be found in *Nine Tales of Raven* by Fran Martin (New York: Harper and Row, 1951) 31-37.